D1548721

Love is
a time of enchantment:
in it all days are fair and all fields
green. Youth is blest by it,
old age made benign: the eyes of love see
roses blooming in December,
and sunshine through rain. Verily
is the time of true-love
a time of enchantment — and
Oh! how eager is woman
to be bewitched!

MOON ISLAND

Emma Read went to the island as
governess to a group of unruly children
to whom she gradually became a friend.
But her employer's stern demeanour
towards her never relaxed. Not easily
scared, Emma began to wonder what
was the secret of the blonde woman
who appeared only on the castle roof.
With her life in danger, Emma set out
to find the truth behind the beauty of
Moon Island and its castle. In so doing
she discovered the happiness she had
longed for with a man she loved.

Books by Kay Winchester
in the Ulverscroft Library:

LOVE FOR DR. PENN
DOCTOR PAUL'S PATIENT
DESTINED FOR YOU
THE NARROW BRIDGE
CLOUDS ON THE MOON
NO EASY ROAD
LOVE COMES SECRETLY
NURSE DRAKE'S DILEMMA
DR SHAW'S SECRETARY
PASSPORT TO PARADISE
NURSE ROWAN'S RETURN

KAY WINCHESTER

MOON ISLAND

Complete and Unabridged

ULVERSCROFT
Leicester

First published in Great Britain in 1973 by
Robert Hale & Company
London

First Large Print Edition
published March 1991

British Library CIP Data

Winchester, Kay, *1913 –*
    Moon Island. – Large print ed. –
    Ulverscroft large print series: romance
    I. Title
    823.914

    ISBN 0–7089–2399–2

Published by
F. A. Thorpe (Publishing) Ltd.
Anstey, Leicestershire
Set by Words & Graphics Ltd.
Anstey, Leicestershire
Printed and bound in Great Britain by
T. J. Press (Padstow) Ltd., Padstow, Cornwall

1

IT was a blazing hot day in July when I made the train journey to Layborough, where I was to change for the coast and Moon Island. Like me, the rest of the passengers seemed to be from schools. Small boys in uniform rushed up and down the corridor and two sixth formers in the corner were trying to pretend they had left their uniform behind, because they so badly wanted to catch the eye of the young man facing me. I had left my uniform behind, because I had left school. I was over age, anyway, and had only stayed over time to suit the staff, because the headmistress had been so kind to me in helping me with my future career. Nursing, at St John's Hospital. I didn't look with inviting approval at the young man in the corner. He was a doctor. I could see that much on the back of the letter he was reading, and on his luggage labels, so interest in him could wait. What I wanted to see was my last glimpse of St John's until the end of the summer holidays.

There it was. I craned forward sharply and stood for a better view, forgetting the adult air I had been carefully trying to acquire, and the mature appearance of my new grey suit and silk shirt. I followed the glimpse of the hospital until it was out of sight; a stark new building of cement and glass and chromium, but all terribly efficient and well equipped. I knew that — I had been escorted over it twice and I had done voluntary work in my spare time, pushing the trolley shop and doing the flowers. Anything, to get into a hospital and see what went on.

The young man facing me appeared amused. "Now what is so interesting about our very ugly new hospital?" he asked.

"I'm going to be a nurse there," I said, and added, "Doctor," because that made it sound more professional and brought the whole thing nearer.

"Oh. Are you, indeed?" he asked, in an altered tone. Now I had his interest, and the two sixth formers in the corner knew it wasn't worth bothering any further. At the next stop they got out, anyway. I didn't even notice their going. I was too busy telling him all about my future. Just talking about it made it seem more real.

"It's a beastly nuisance that I couldn't go last year but I was under age," I explained. "But I've been a cadet nurse in my holidays. I've learned quite a lot," and for some reason he encouraged me to tell him just how much I did know. I didn't watch the telephone poles flash by any more, nor did I notice that the schoolboys thinned out along the way until we were alone in the compartment. I liked talking about it and he liked listening.

"So you're an orphan, and you think you want to make your life in hospital," he said at last, and he looked at me. I wondered if he were thinking that because I had no glamour or raving good looks, and that because I was so neat and well-groomed, that I was the stuff of which ward sisters were made. I hoped so.

"I've always wanted to be a nurse," I told him, and I thought how marvellous it would be if it turned out that he were the houseman at St John's. I hadn't dared ask. All the doctors and surgeons I had seen there were not as young as he was, or else callow youths just scrambling through their last year of training, and doing it for the job. He somehow looked dedicated. He had a thin sensitive face, and nice grey eyes, neatly cut light brown hair, and good looks that must surely be satisfying to sick patients.

"And you know, of course, that you won't be allowed to touch a patient for at least two years — beyond the menial tasks, of course?" he said, very seriously.

I agreed that I did know. "I've read up all about it and asked people. I know I shall have to start at the bottom again in the Preliminary Training School, in spite of all the things I've already learnt, and I know that in some ways a junior nurse is only a glorified housemaid, but I don't care. I want to be *in* it. Seeing things done for people. I just want to be in the world of hospital. Does that sound very juvenile?"

"No, not at all," he said, very gently. "I wish you all the success and the luck in the world. I hope you will be very happy. Not everyone is, you know, who works in hospital."

"How can they be otherwise?" I asked blankly. I was absolutely sure in my own mind that nobody could be unhappy doing such a worthwhile job.

"Oh, I don't know. I wished you luck. I think luck plays a very big part, you know. Some people, with the best will in the world, don't find their heart's desire working in hospital. I could tell you quite a few stories . . . but I won't. I couldn't bear to disillusion you so soon. But do bear it in mind. You might just not find the happiness there that you're so sure you will. Anyway, so for the moment you're going on holiday?" and he twisted round to try and read my luggage label.

"It's a working holiday," I told him. "I haven't got anyone belonging to me. There isn't much left, now my education's paid for, so it seemed the best idea. It ought to be fun. I'm going to a place called Moon Island."

The name had an odd effect on him. He jerked back from his efforts to read my luggage labels, and ejaculated: "Good heavens!"

"What does that mean?" I asked him.

He sat staring out of the window, and only when I repeated my question, could I get an answer out of him.

"I think I know the owner," he said,

in a queer voice. Then he pulled himself together. "Well, who are you staying with? Who will you be working for?"

I got out the letter with all the arrangements in it. "I'm going to work for a Mrs Boyd. Companion, secretary, general factotum. Whatever she wants me to do, that the staff don't or won't do," I said, with a smile. It had sounded rather fun.

"There you have me. I don't know the lady. I take it you won't be actually living at Moon House."

"Oh, yes. Yes, I shall," I said. "You know this island? What's it like?"

He smiled rather tenderly at the eagerness in my tones. I must have sounded gauche. I could see my reflection in the train window, with my neat boyish haircut and fringe, light brown hair a little darker than thick honey. Hazel eyes and very dark straight lashes, and a very, very determined chin. That chin was almost but not quite square. And I had thought I looked soignee and grown-up!

"You'll like it, I expect," he said, with sudden comfort in his tones. "Yes, I think you'll like it," as if he thought other girls might not. "It's a beauty spot," he threw in as an afterthought.

"Oh, then I expect there'll be a lot of summer visitors. Does Moon House — ?"

"It does not!" he sounded shocked. "No visitors allowed on the island. And Moon House is as impregnable as a castle. Haven't you been told? The chap who owns it writes, or something. Seldom seen. Something of a recluse. And no one! But no one — goes over that causeway without a good reason, like tradesmen and so on."

"Oh." I felt rather dashed.

He hastened to say, "Oh, look, don't let me spoil it for you. It really is a lovely place. If you like swimming and walking, or boating, well, it's got the lot. The last time I was there, the house was shut up and empty. That was when I was a student. There was some talk of the house being sold for a hotel. It would make a wonderful holiday spot. Then it passed into other hands when the old chap died, and now it's very much the home of a recluse. That's all."

And to soften the picture he had drawn of the place, he began to quietly tell me about it and about that stretch of rather wild undeveloped coast. He, it seemed, was going to stay with a friend, in Chighampton, farther down, where there was sailing to be had, and fishing, the things he liked best.

I suppose it was appropriate for it to have happened, on my first day away from the sheltering arm of school. I was stunned by the unexpectedness of it. There we were, the train purring along, and Dr Pearce telling me about the view of Moon Island in the moonlight, or at dawn, when it was just a long grey smudge on a pearly sea, when suddenly his voice was blotted out by a collection of raucous sound — screeching of train brakes, the splintering of wood, the cries of people, and a jolt that threw me past him on to the far seat. Our carriage rocked dangerously for a moment or two and then stayed still, tilted on end.

I heard his voice. "Are you all right?" We hadn't got round to exchanging names yet. I said in a shaken voice, "I — I think so. Are you? Where are you, doctor?"

There was a shuddering of the carriage and some luggage fell as he pulled himself out from under the debris. I couldn't see him clearly at first, because the dust was still rising. His hair was no longer tidy, and

8

he had a trickle of blood running down one side of his face, which he wiped off with the back of his hand.

He got me out from under an upturned seat, hastily ran his hands over me and pronounced no bones broken. "Now — you want to be a nurse. Now's your chance — or don't you feel up to it?"

I said indignantly that of course I did (though I didn't) and he said, "Good girl! I'm Nolan Pearce, by the way."

"I'm Emma Read."

"Then, Emma Read, come along and help me. They'll need help," he said.

I grew up that day. I had gone on that train as a recent schoolgirl, now straining to pretend to be grown-up. After I had helped Nolan Pearce, and the nursing sisters who had come with the ambulances, the doctors from the hospitals in a wide arc and some nuns from a Catholic hospital very near, I didn't have to pretend to be grown-up.

It was the usual level-crossing accident, but previously I had only read about them in the papers and wondered what it could be like and why someone should be somehow involved with a train, when driving a car. Now it didn't matter why.

It was a question of (for me) helping those who could manage to walk, to those ambulances which were packing in the slightly injured, and the experienced people were attending to the badly hurt. But at the last, I crawled in a small place to get at someone that bigger people couldn't manage. I didn't have to. I just found I could get through and I went. Nolan shone a torch in and told me what to do while we were waiting for the gigantic machine with the acetylene cutter to remove some of the smashed carriage to get the injured out.

It got very confused at that point. I was taken to one hospital with some other people to be treated for shock. I didn't see what happened to Nolan but I heard someone say that Dr Pearce had had some heavy debris fall on his leg and had been taken back to St John's. The day raced by, and I had lost my luggage — all I had in the world was in that case. I tried to find out about Nolan Pearce's condition and I was promised word if I waited for an hour. Then I tried to telephone the island to tell them why I would be late but I learned that they weren't on the telephone. So with a lot of patience I finally got through to the nearest shop on the mainland, which was in a place called King's Dassett, and they said someone would be going out to the island that day with some stores and would take the message.

I had done my best. Now I had to get myself to Moon Island. The sky was draining itself of colour and light when I had my first bit of luck. Someone had found my suitcase. It was slashed across the top, and the side stove in, but my things were intact. I got a later train beyond the level crossing, but by the time I changed at Layborough and got some form of transport to King's Dassett, it was dark.

King's Dassett didn't look much of a place at night. Its little streets wound about. I found the General Store but it was closed. A head came out of the top window and asked what I wanted.

I said, "I have to go out to Moon Island. How can I get there?"

It was a very old woman. She said no one listened to her, so it was no good her saying, but if it was her wanting such an outlandish thing as to go to Moon Island, she would use her own legs and march herself over the causeway, pretty smartly, she added, on account of the tide would be rising any minute. Then she banged down the window and I couldn't make her raise it again.

I couldn't imagine how one found the causeway. I couldn't even hear the sound of the sea. I humped my battered case, and changed my shoulder bag to the other side. I looked a mess. They had done their best to clean off the bloodstains at the hospital, but my one new suit was ruined. I had to pass the pub. It was just a small house, joined to all the others, with a swinging sign. The King's Head.

It was still open. The light was bright, but there was a lot of noise, singing and laughing and the clinking of glasses. I was suddenly reluctant to go in.

An elderly man came out, however, and offered to take me to the causeway. He looked like a fisherman and wore a woolly cap that had seen better days. He said, "Stranger in these parts," and glanced at my battered case.

"I've been in a train accident. I'm going to work on Moon Island."

"Oh, aye. Reckon I'd best take you to

the island, then, but I'll have to ask you to wait till the tide comes in." He scratched his head. "See, if I goes on foot with you, miss, I'll be too late to walk back."

My heart sank. What would they say on the island? I asked him if my message had been delivered. "I gave it to the telephone operator." That made him laugh, and he explained that the old woman in the general store was also the telephone operator and postmistress, and she only sent messages if she felt like it, and she certainly wouldn't send one to the island since Mary Abbott had upset her.

"Who's Mary Abbott?" I asked, wondering what Mrs Boyd must be thinking.

"Why, she's Oliver Cripley's married daughter. She does for 'em up at Moon House," and then he didn't say any more, because we turned yet another bend in the winding lane, and there were no more hedges and trees, only scrub, wasteland down to the beach, dunes, and wet hard ripply sand, and a cobbled causeway all the way out to the island.

Moonlight splayed kindly over it all. It was quite breathtaking. I just stood and stared in delight at it. I remembered

13

thinking, bruised and battered and shocked as I had been that day, that here was my reward at the end. I also thought that the island was a very romantic place to work on.

The fisherman beside me exploded all that tranquillity and fanciful dreaming. "Ah, now, miss, see that dark smudge on the causeway out there? It's a man, coming this way. Reckon on it being Mr Stanton, looking for you. Best get your right foot forward, miss. He won't be pleased. You don't need me now. I'll wish you goodnight." And the way he said it, I knew this would be the recluse!

He left me, without another word, so I hustled. It wasn't easy. The soft fine sand got in my shoes, and now that I was down there at the place where the water would begin, it wasn't easy to find the causeway in this faint light.

It wasn't very easy walking on it when I did find it, either. I did my best, because the distance between that figure we had seen, was lessening alarmingly and I feared I wasn't going to get a very good reception.

He was a very tall man. Tall and lithe as

a whipcord, by the way he strode along. He came up to me and said, "Good heavens! Where the devil have you been and what happened to you?"

It was a cultured voice, the sort that is riddled with authority. I looked up at him, framing an answer. He took my arm and marched me forward. "Tell me as we go — we'll be caught by the tide if we're not careful!"

He took my breath away. The way he spoke to me, it struck me that he might have thought I was a servant and it wouldn't have been a very good way to speak to one of those. At school one had to be very careful not to offend the maids or they left on the instant and then the Head got very cross.

I said with great dignity, "I really couldn't help it, and I did send a message to King's Dassett, to be brought out with the grocery, but I did think Mrs Boyd would understand. It wasn't my fault that the train ran into a car at a level crossing."

He stopped dead for a moment as I said that. Then he took my case from me, and said curtly, "Well, come on. It isn't Mrs Boyd you have to worry about. It's — "

I broke in rather anxiously, "But I'm to be her companion and secretary. Of course I have to worry about her. She'll wonder what's happened to me!"

"What the devil are you talking about?" he demanded, stopping again. "Look here, aren't you Sally Martindale from Chighampton?"

I said, "No, I'm not. I'm Emma Read, and I'm here for the school holidays, and then I'm going back to St John's Hospital, to train as a nurse."

That made me feel a little more confident, but the confidence was brief. I caught a glimpse of his face. He looked horrified.

"Was this Sally Martindale a friend or a visitor or something?" I asked.

"No, she was not. She was the new maid. She'll be the third who didn't arrive. But why on earth Mrs Boyd should need a companion, beats me," he muttered, and he sounded very angry indeed.

It was almost dark by the time we reached the island. The sea was running in, silently, with almost no foam at the edges. Just a little sinister because of the darkness and the strangeness of it all. We went up a lot of steps. I was weary by then, but the steps had to be climbed.

There were a lot of trees, so far as I could see in the darkness, and the rising wind whispered through them. My guide hurried me on, across a courtyard, through a door in the wall, along passages, and then there was the house. Moon House. Built to last, because in winter this place would be buffeted by the elements. That was the impression I got, mainly because the coldness of the stone walls rose to meet me.

But inside, with the doors shut against the darkness and the wind, I was aware of a certain shabbiness of drapery in the revealing light from a collection of lamps that, when pumped up, gave off almost as powerful a light as electricity. The furniture was old and solid, but a lot needed doing to the place, and nobody came to attend to the door or to answer a bell. We stood there for a moment, and in the silence I heard a woman's tread; firm, unhurried. She was in her late forties, casually but smartly dressed in a two-piece, with a good hair set suggesting she wasn't touched by this need for money.

17

She looked at me, and then at the tall young man beside me. Waiting, it seemed, to take her cue from him. Then she suddenly realized that the state I was in, hadn't resulted from the stains of an ordinary journey. "My dear, whoever you are, what on earth happened to you?" she cried in concern.

"I'm Emma Read, and I'm sorry I'm so late but they did promise in King's Dassett to deliver my message from the hospital. I got involved with a level crossing accident — my train collided with a car."

So I had to tell the story all over again. Mrs Boyd was sympathetic, but practical, too. She took charge, which gave the taciturn Mr Stanton a chance to escape with an angry snort at the women's combined chatter.

Mrs Boyd had me out of my stained clothes and into a warm bath in no time, and there was a good light meal and fragrant coffee waiting for me, to have in my dressing-gown in my room.

Mrs Boyd said, "It's only a small room, I'm afraid, and you may be required to do some clerical work in here, which is why I provided a writing table. But I'm sure you'll find the job an interesting one for your summer holidays."

I thanked her and ate. I couldn't remember when I had ate last, now I came to think of it. I was starving, and after that tray-load I felt lots better.

"About Mr Stanton," I began, hesitantly.

"Yes?" she asked guardedly.

"Well, it was rather odd. A man from the village had promised to bring me out to the island and then he said there was no need as he could see Mr Stanton coming. But when Mr Stanton reached me he appeared to think I was a maid called Sally Martindale from Chighampton, and when I explained who I was, he didn't seem to think you needed a companion and he seemed very angry. I didn't know what to do."

"Oh, he was bothered about the silly girl not turning up, in case she got drowned, not knowing about the tides, you see. I told him not to expect a maid would come from Chighampton to work here — it stands to reason. Chighampton is a bright, popular resort. The girls prefer to work there. But he would insist on advertising for servants. No, we shall just have to go on making do with people from the village, which is handy for them, just crossing the causeway. Don't think another thing about it."

"You mean he knew I was to come?"

"Not necessarily," she said cheerfully. "He very often doesn't bother to listen to what I say. It doesn't matter. You're here, and after you've had a good night's sleep, we'll talk about your duties. Of course, as we can't seem to get a maid, it would be a help if you would do a few little odd jobs. You'll get plenty of time off for swimming and boating or anything else you like, of course."

After she had left me, I snuggled down in a really comfortable bed; a bed three times the size of the one I had had at my boarding-school. And what she called a smallish room was quite a large room after what I had been used to. With the lamp out, and the moonlight coming in at the window, I determined to think of all the things that had happened to me that day but I didn't, after all. The sound of the tide not far away, and the keen fresh night air coming in at the open window, sent me into a deep sleep until the morning.

Morning on the island was sheer beauty.

There was a pearly sheen on the sea and the mainland was hidden in mist. It would be another hot day. Somewhere near at hand there were chickens making soft noises, and someone's voice scolding in the kitchen. It was still only six o'clock. I thought I had better not get up yet. Mrs Boyd must be asked for bathroom times. I didn't think I could find my way to the bathroom anyway, without further directions. It had seemed a twisty, confused path she had led me to and from that beautiful steamy hot bath last night, in a room that had once been a bedroom before its conversion.

Still, the thought of the bathroom and perhaps a dip in that sea, sent me on a path of exploration which I was sorry for. I got lost, and finished up on a railed balcony at the end of the house. Dense dark trees hemmed in this end of the house, and it seemed rather gloomy. I was about to turn back when I heard my name mentioned, from a room above. I looked up and saw another railed balcony similar to the one I was standing on, and the glass doors behind it were open. Mrs Boyd said, "She seems a nice girl and if you don't keep on behaving as if you had the blackest secret in the world that you were hiding, I can't see that she should be suspicious."

Mr Stanton's voice cracked back with the sharpness of a whip. "I would say that that is just what I have got, and it is necessary to protect it, and if you would only speak to me before you import strangers here . . . "

"Well, for goodness sake, what are the maids you hire, if not strangers?" Mrs Boyd asked mildly. From what I remembered of her last night — comfortably fat, with light brown eyes that beamed unquestionably at everyone and a mild round face that suggested very good temper, to say the least — she really wouldn't mind if maids came or they didn't. I imagined she would ignore a film of dust or wilting flowers, so long as her own person was neat and well-groomed.

"That is not the case at all," Mr Stanton snapped. "The maids stay in the kitchen. This girl, by reason of her duties (if that is what they can be called) will be here, there and everywhere. Moreover, she tells me she wants to be a nurse at a hospital."

"Why, that's splendid!" Mrs Boyd said

happily. "What more can you want?"

"I'll tell you what more I can want — her departure, right away. She has the rebel look about her — "

" — what, *that* quiet, mild-looking child?" Mrs Boyd broke in.

Mr Stanton was silent for a moment, while he tamped down his temper, I imagined. "Yes, that mild-looking child," he said at last. "Oh, I grant you she looks quiet, but I know her type. She's a righter of wrongs, a would-be dedicated healer of the sick. I've seen them before in the P.T.S. Sister Tutor invites them with open arms but everyone else shrinks with horror at their energy and their inquisitive ways. Make no mistake, they are all inquisitive, in case there's a crusade for them which is being hidden. And I don't want such a person here. My heavens, the occupant of the top floor would explode, for a start!"

Mrs Boyd said. "Yes, you have a point there, if you are right. But I don't think you are. Anyway, Miss Read need not worry you. I've got her mainly for a companion."

"Why should you want a companion?" he demanded.

23

"Because," Mrs Boyd said softly, coming to the window so quickly that I had to duck back in case I was discovered, "in spite of this being a beautiful paradise, I get so lonely and bored, I could scream at times. I hope she will provide companionship in return for the meagre pay we're offering her."

I felt slightly sick. I shouldn't have listened to any of that, but I had heard my name mentioned, and I couldn't go away. What on earth was I to do now? Mrs Boyd wanted me but he didn't, and it would seem that he was the owner of this place, the boss — the recluse, surely, that Dr Pearce had spoken of yesterday?

Nice Nolan Pearce, nice ordinary normal Nolan Pearce, was a long way away and I missed him. I shot down the corridor again and searched for the bathroom, this time finding it and memorizing the way, and as I took a cold shower, I promised myself I'd get over to the mainland to telephone the hospital to find out how he was. He had seemed friendly enough on the train. I hoped his friendship would ripen. I could do with a friend.

Mrs Boyd knocked on my door just as I

had finished dressing. She had a breakfast tray with her.

"Oh, but you mustn't wait on me," I protested. I could feel my face growing hot with embarrassment. Was this the way they intended to keep me in one place so that I didn't discover the secret?

Mrs Boyd smiled. "I didn't do it. I just took the tray from Mary Abbott to save her time. In this house we are so much dependent on staff and as you have already heard, they are so hard to come by, so we have to pamper them, and Mary Abbott won't have people taking breakfast downstairs. We all have to have it in our rooms. It leaves the dining-room untouched for lunch and the evening meal. You will remember not to make extra work for the staff, won't you?"

I nodded, and sat down rather weakly. Mrs Boyd said, "Eat it in comfort, and afterwards, come to my room — at the end of the corridor above this — and we'll talk about your duties."

Well, I knew where her room was, didn't I? And what was the owner doing in it at six o'clock in the morning?

My conscience started to worry me, and

it didn't stop. It ruined that good breakfast of coffee, toast, kidneys and eggs and bacon, and marmalade. I still couldn't quell my conscience, even after I had taken the tray and put it on the table Mrs Boyd had told me I should find. There it would be collected by Mrs Abbott when she collected everyone else's, and there was someone from the village who would be waiting to do the washing up.

I kept thinking of the size of the house and the work there was to do, all the way up to Mrs Boyd's room. I wasn't grown-up. I was just a sixth former still, worried about my latest escapade, and anxious only to tell the headmistress and get it off my chest. I despised myself. I told myself that it would be worse if I told Mrs Boyd I had eavesdropped. What degree of trust could there be, if she was to learn that at the start of our association? Much better leave it at the accident it had been, and not let her know.

She was such a nice person. She even managed to look a little shamefaced when she listed all the things she hoped I would do, to 'help out'.

"I wouldn't ask it if I wasn't really hard

pressed," she apologized.

"That's all right. I don't mind," I said. "Actually it will give me a chance to get used to hard work because I'm going to work in a hospital immediately I leave here."

"Yes, I know," she said. "May I ask what made you decide you wanted to take up nursing?"

"I always wanted to," I said.

"The accident yesterday must have been very unpleasant for you. Didn't that tend to put you off?"

"Not at all. In fact, afterwards I was even more anxious to get at the job. If things like that are happening all the time, then people like me must be needed all the time."

"That's true," she said, undoubtedly thinking of other things. I wondered whose idea it had been to give me the jobs a maid would normally do, and clerical work thrown in, just for the pittance a paid companion — a temporary one at that — could command. Of course, they were exploiting me. I should be paid three times what they were offering. True, I was to live in a beauty spot, but I shouldn't get much time to enjoy it, by the look of it.

She got up. "Will you decide now, please, if you feel you can agree to do all those things, because if not, it might be better if you go somewhere else. I know some people who just want someone for odd jobs, and a lot of time to spare, really just a few odd jobs," she added hastily, as my eyebrows went up. "This job is really putting on you. I didn't realize it until I told you what I wanted you to do."

That, of course, made me like her, made me want to stay. I said so.

She looked almost tearful in her relief. "Well, I'm more glad than I can say, because to be frank, Mr Stanton wasn't pleased." She looked as if she wanted to say something else, but decided against it. "Come along and see the rest of the house and get your bearings. You found my room pretty well."

That was my chance, and me being me, I just had to take it. "I know I did, but there was a reason," I said desperately. "I knew it at six this morning when I was searching for the bathroom. I stood under your balcony and heard all you said."

I watched her feel for the back of the chair behind her and hold it, lower herself

28

into it. She looked fussed, bothered. Her face blanched, and she never took her eyes off mine. "What did you hear me say?" she whispered.

I told her. "I didn't mean to listen, but it's automatic, isn't it, when you hear your own name mentioned, and then it went too far and I couldn't move away. Besides, if you don't mind me saying so, I was a bit worried as to why the owner was in your room at that early hour. It's not very nice to put it so bluntly but it's my first job and I've got no family to look after me and, well, it looked sort of queer."

Well, there it was. It was said. I waited for her to throw me out. She didn't though. She looked at the table cover and said, in a preoccupied way, "Oh, that? Is that all? Heywood Stanton's my son, by a former marriage."

That knocked the breath out of me, as no doubt she intended it to. Well, if that were true, then why shouldn't a son drift into his mother's bedroom and have an argument with her, and what better time than at six, before the household was up and about? It explained, too, why she said so casually last night the things she had, about maids and companions. She had seemed too sure of herself to be the housekeeper, and now I knew: she was his mother. And what had I been gauche enough to suggest?

I stumbled over apologies, which she waived away, and we did a tour of the house, and in the embarrassment of my suggestion, I forgot to ask her about the remark about 'the occupant of the top floor'. So far as I could see, the top floor was full of rooms that might have been servants bedrooms in better days, and there was a sewing-room with a treadle machine, a dress model, a full-length mirror, and some curtains in the making. She said if I was interested in making my own clothes, I could use the room. There was also a dark-room for photography, and a room fitted up with various musical instruments, a battery-run player and shelves of records. "Sound-proof," she said, "while my son is working in his study down below. You can use the room if you want to."

There were reasonably well kept kitchen gardens, a walled garden where strawberries were grown, marrows on their piles of straw, cucumbers under frames. "Who does all this?" I asked in surprise.

"Mary Abbott's brother," she said collectedly. It seemed that the people on the island were all inter-married and largely formed the staff. Then why send away to Chighampton for a maid?

"Do you know anything about gardening?" she asked me.

"No, but I'm willing to learn. I want to learn about everything," I said, and offered, "I can do shorthand and typing."

That delighted her.

"But that's marvellous. You could help my son — that's if you didn't mind," she said, going pink at the thought of putting something else on me. "Well, typing costs the earth to send it out."

"What does he write? Fiction?" I wanted to know.

"No, actually history. It's the only thing that interests him now."

That of course left it open for me to ask what he had been interested in before, but there was that in her manner which made more questions untenable.

That day I got through shelling the peas for Mary Abbott in a kitchen that would have done very well in a monastery — all stonework, stark simplicity, the total absence of gadgetry, even of light. The smallest window lighted it. I wiped up mountains of crockery, then helped Mrs Boyd to answer some letters. They weren't very interesting. Some were to solicitors, discussing repairs that needed doing at once, and others looming for the future. She wrote to stores in London, discussing purchases by mail, and she wrote a guarded letter to someone in Poltoncross called 'Darrell'. She said she would address that letter herself.

After lunch, at which Heywood didn't appear, she asked me if I would walk across the causeway and do some shopping for her. She wanted more stamps, some sewing cotton and to ask if any parcels had come for her by the late post. "We usually sent to London for whatever we want, but I thought you might like to see the General Store in King's Dassett and buy any little things you needed, and you need not be back until tea-time." That just gave me time for half an hour's exploring of the island, I thought, with pleasure.

I took a basket and went off. But I missed the way that I was brought in last night and I expect she forgot to tell me. Instead I found myself down in the main street of the island, where there were a few cottages, and some grubby children sitting on one of the doorsteps.

They were a boy of about ten, a girl of about seven and another boy who could have been six. They had such intelligent faces, they should have been cleaned up and given something useful to do. I supposed that that was how the islanders got, in a place like this. The girl's jersey was torn, the boys had jagged holes in their shorts, and buttons missing off their shirts. I said to them, "Where does the causeway start?"

They all looked deadpan, as if a switch had been pressed. I repeated the question, and then the children looked at each other, and the little boy pointed, down an alley between two cottages. It didn't look right, but they should know — they lived here.

I went down the passage. It smelt nasty of dustbins and stale cooking. A cat sat high on the wall with a sleepy pair of amber eyes. As I passed, it shot out a paw in a half-hearted attempt to scratch at me. I stopped and tried to make friends with it but it took umbrage and walked with majesty up the tiles to the top roof.

It had distracted my attention. I walked on, looking round at the cat, and almost came to a terrifying end. There was what appeared to be an open gate in a fence. The gate wasn't on the fence. It was standing against the wall. Someone had been putting a new hinge on. Below the gate, there was a half flight of wooden steps, the half that were nearest the beach. The top half had gone. There was a sheer drop, enough to hurt someone badly, if not kill them.

A man called out, "Hey, there, look out! Them little varmints have moved the guard again! I'll tell 'em something. Could have been narsty. You want to watch where you're going, miss."

It gave me a bad turn, but when I recovered, I went back to find the children. They had gone. Later, I found the bigger boy, looking innocently down at the causeway, a snake-like path to the shore made of rounded white stones, green in places from the sea, but quite beautiful in its way. I looked at it too, then remembered the part the boy had played and wanted to box his ears. "Do you know I could have had a very nasty accident? What made you send me down to those broken steps?" I fumed.

"But I didn't," he said with reason.

"Well, you let the little boy tell me!"

"No, I didn't. That was Timmy. He's always pointing. Nobody takes any notice of him! I was going to tell you the way, but you walked off."

So that was how it was going to be. "Listen," I warned him, "any more nonsense and I shall tell Mrs Boyd."

He considered the point gravely. "She won't do anything," he said at last, with such telling conviction that I jumped to the conclusion he must be belonging to Mary Abbott, a person whose services they were so lucky to get. I conceded the point, and left him, to go down on to the causeway.

He called down after me. "Know the time of the tide?"

I didn't want him giving me the wrong time, for sure, so I told him I did, and didn't need his help.

He looked at me with the same look the cat had; bland until that wicked paw had come down to swipe me. He said, "If you're going into the Post Office for Mrs Boyd ask for Cotton Dodgers."

I paused. "What are they?"

He shrugged. "Don't ask, if you don't want to. Nothing in my life. Just thought I'd offer the information."

So I thought he was trying to make up for the first thing that had gone wrong, and decided to ask for it. Really, I should have had more sense than to think he was belonging to Mary Abbott. His voice was the voice of a boy at boarding school, totally without the local accent that Mary Abbott and the man repairing the steps had had. But I didn't think just then.

I went over the causeway and into the Post Office and bought the stamps. The old woman gravely put off the headphones and left the exchange to come and serve me. She took her position seriously. It was a jolly nice little shop. Like every place hereabouts, there was the inevitable flight of steps up to the front door, and the rooms were very small, and there was a front garden laden with cottagey flowers. The drone of the bees made me feel sleepy and I asked clearly for Cotton Dodgers.

I really thought it was some kind of local reel of cotton. There were three women talking in the shop. They broke off and went into gales of laughter, and went to the door and shouted to some more people. They passed it on, screaming with mirth, until it seemed that the whole village was laughing at me, and the post mistress was going into a frenzy, trying to hit out at me with a telephone book she had picked up. "Cheeky young miss from London!" she kept shouting. "Bad as them kids on the island!"

Only then did I see that I had again been the victim of those children and their unholy sense of humour. As soon as I could, I went back to the island, my walk forgotten, and searched for them. But of course, they had gone into hiding.

What on earth was I going to do now? Nobody would listen when I had tried to explain how I had come to mention Cotton Dodgers. Nobody would say what Cotton Dodgers were or why the post mistress got so wrathful at their being mentioned. I supposed I would find out later.

Meanwhile, I could at least tackle Mary Abbott, who was coming towards me, looking anything but pleased. Personally I didn't care if I did upset her. I said, "Mrs Abbott, your children have played two bad tricks on me today and one might have cost me my life."

She lifted gloomy eyes to mine. "I haven't got any children, young miss. My man went to sea ten years ago and I've not seen him since.

I was covered in horror and confusion. I stammered apologies and explained which children I meant and what they had done. A gleam of malice came into her eyes when I mentioned 'Cotton Dodgers' but I didn't ask her what it was. I just said bluntly, "Then whose children are they because I have something to say to the parents!"

"You'd best take your complaint to Mrs Boyd," she said, and passed me.

I hesitated to do that, but I hadn't brought the sewing cotton back and something would have to be said. She came to find me, in the end, with a plea for me to help with the mending in that upstairs room. She was snowed under with sheets. She said she had enough cotton to go on with, if I'd get some the next day, and again I cowardly shelved the question of Cotton Dodgers. But I did tell her about the steps.

She was shocked. "Who *are* those children? Where are their parents?" I asked her, but she just shook her head.

"Oh, dear, this is awful," she murmured. "They have no parents. As a matter of fact, they have recently lost their father in rather tragic circumstances. They don't know about it. I mean, they just know he died. I am letting them think he was just ill. But for the moment they are our responsibility."

"You mean, they live here?"

She nodded. "It was rather cowardly of me. I should have mentioned them. But I've asked you to do so much, and actually I wanted you to give part of your time to, well, giving an eye to them. They don't need looking after, in the sense of a nursemaid. They are very self-sufficient children!"

"Self-sufficient!" I exploded, and thought about the way they had sat looking at me, with their deadpan faces, while the little boy pointed the way to certain death. Had it just been a trick on that youngster's part? Or had they already seen me about, recognized me as a gullible stranger and planned it ready to try out on me? Surely not! "Their mischief could be dangerous," I said. "Are they often — " and then I broke off. I didn't want to have to admit what a fool I had been to fall into the trap of the Cotton Dodgers. I really should have known better than that, and there had been no danger in that trick.

"I don't know what they're like, really," Mrs Boyd said worriedly. "I have my own anxieties. In the short while they have been here, I'm afraid I've left them to their own devices. Mary Abbott sees to their material needs. She always wanted children of her own, you know. I thought she'd like to do it."

"But isn't this island a dangerous place for young children who are strangers to it?" I asked her.

She smiled gently. "Well, that is why I needed someone like you to give an eye to them when you can," she explained.

I began to feel sorry for the taciturn owner of this place. With such a mother, he had troubles enough. She was so nice, so kind, but so winsome when she wanted her own way. I was quite sure he couldn't stand out against her in a crisis. He might bully other people, but not her. She was the sort who got her own way with any young man.

More than ever, I wished I could get into

touch with Dr Pearce and have the benefit of his good sense. I longed to tell him what it was like here and to ask his advice, and I had forgotten to ring the hospital today, in my wrath against the children.

That would have to wait. I couldn't get to the mainland just yet. There was work that Mr Stanton wanted help with, his mother said.

I wondered that he could bring himself to accept help from me, after all he had said, but as soon as I had finished helping her with the mending, I went along and tapped at the study door.

He looked less stiff and formal than last night. He had neat grey slacks and a fine sweater of a slightly lighter shade, and he was lighting a pipe when he invited me to go in. It struck me that he had got himself eased out with his work, and that the sight of me banished all that. His eyebrows shot up and he asked uncompromisingly. "What do *you* want?"

"Your mother said you needed some help. I can type and do some shorthand," I said, trying to keep quiet and polite.

"You do both?" he demanded, and when I nodded agreement, he sat back in his chair and asked bluntly, "Then if you're so good at so many things, what are you wasting your time here for?"

"I'm beginning to wonder," I snapped, forgetting the most important maxim my mother had left me. Then I apologized. It's no good starting off on the wrong foot. "I was given this job as a holiday task, and I'm determined to do the best I can with it, never mind what I'm paid for it. It's a lovely place to be in, anyway."

He considered that answer, and finally nodded. "All right, sit down. Know anything about history?"

"Well, it depends on the period," I said, studying him. "I prefer Roman times but we seemed to do the last three centuries at school, to the extinction of everything else."

His eyes gleamed. They were disconcertingly light eyes in such a darkly tanned face, and he was so virile — and tensed. Tensed all the time. I had noticed it before. I said, with a view to putting him at his ease, "If I hadn't come here to Moon Island for my holiday job, I had made up my mind to try and get attached to some 'dig' somewhere, as a sort of general helper, so that I could have the benefit of history, and open air too, if you see what I mean."

"Well, you won't get much history here," he said shortly. "I understand you were engaged to help the kitchen staff, save my mother from boredom, and watch to see that the children didn't do irreparable damage to a place already falling to bits."

"If you mean this house, it doesn't look so bad to me. I thought it was a wonderful old house, when I arrived last night," I said.

"You're being kind," he told me. "I'd rather you spoke your mind. The place is falling to bits. Let's let it rest at that."

So he was determined to be on unfriendly terms with me! I mentally shrugged and turned my attention to the work he had given me. It wasn't very easy. It was pages of notes in someone's awful handwriting, waiting to be typed. The machine was quite ancient, a real wrist-breaker. But I persevered, and from my wide reading of Roman finds, I was able to make some sense of the stuff. And I didn't take too long with it.

He grunted in what might almost have

been approval when I turned it in to him. "Like doing this sort of thing?" he jerked at me.

I said I did. It was true. I had found it interesting.

"As I said before, I would prefer you to be blunt," he said. "Of course you didn't find it interesting, seated in a dark room with the sun and the wind calling from outside. Go on, cut along and find those kids and get some fresh air. And don't do anything dangerous. There's no one with any time to come looking for you!"

Mrs Boyd was crossing the hall when I came out of the study. She waited for me. "Well, how did it go? Did you do some shorthand?"

I told her what I had done.

"And you didn't like it," she concluded, quite erroneously. "Well, my dear, you look very cross."

"That was because your son was determined to . . . no, I shouldn't say that. It's not polite. But I do feel he might have given me a chance to show what I could do first."

"He has a lot to put up with," she said mildly. "Run along and get some fresh air.

Have a swim if you like. Take the children with you."

The children, always the children. I went to find them with no great enthusiasm, but no one appeared to know where they were.

I went through the main street of the island, and asked Mary Abbott, her father who was mending nets, and two other elderly men engaged on painting the hull of a fishing craft. They seemed glad they hadn't seen the children.

I went on a tour of exploration. I might as well see the island, and no one was going to show me, that was clear.

The far side of the island from the mainland was rather a surprise. Here the beach was pitted with large rocks, and cliffs rose to tier over a bay that was only accessible at low water. The island was bigger than I had at first thought. I wasn't going to be able to walk all over it before the children were fetched back for their meal, that was certain. But where, in this wilderness, did one search for three children who, for all I knew, were watching me, hidden somewhere, and would stay out of sight and nip back to the house, leaving me futilely searching?

And then I saw them. The boys were at the top of the cliff. The girl was nowhere to be seen. They were quite near to me really, but I hadn't spotted them because the sun threw long shadows across that part of the cliff. Only a movement from the children had attracted my attention.

My heart started to beat painfully. Was it a trick they were playing on me, or was there something wrong? The big boy was so still, and he looked so anxious. Timmy, the little boy, was trying not to let his face crumple. I looked up in perplexity. "What are you doing up there?" I called up. "You know you're expected back at the house!"

The big boy wouldn't answer, but the little one broke the rules and called out to me. "We're in big trouble," he sobbed.

The big boy turned on him in a fury, but Timmy wouldn't stop. "It's my sister Jenneth. She's caught in the funnel. She's hurt and we daren't let go."

Then I saw they were both holding on to something. Not a rope. More like a thin cord.

I stopped thinking it might be a trick and ran towards them. At the foot of the cliff I could see the girl. She had caught her foot. The cliffs were the crumbling kind. She was hanging on, sheet-white, but her foot was securely jammed in a fissure that had closed up again with falling rubble.

I was no cliff-climber, but one could but try. I called up encouraging things to her, but she didn't answer. She just hung on.

So far as I could see, it wanted someone to go up behind her, hold her, take her weight while her foot was freed. What might happen then, I couldn't think, but they were hanging on to some sort of thin cord, which would stop her from falling.

I did my best. It seemed hours and hours, though it couldn't have been all that long. I kicked for footholds, but my hands were torn and bleeding by the time I reached her. She was a game little thing. She didn't cry, though it must have been a very frightening experience. I discovered to my intense relief, that the blood I had seen was coming from a surface scratch. Her foot wasn't hurt. Once I had taken her weight and undone her shoes, her foot came out easily. We had to leave the shoe behind. There was a rock fall that nearly sent both of us hurling to the bottom. We got ourselves to the top with the help of the cord, and we both collapsed panting on the grass.

I must have blacked out. I was furious. When I came to, the children were sitting round me in a circle. The little girl had lost that ghostly pallor. She was tanned as usual, and her face was deadpan as usual.

I felt terrible. I sat up, livid, and said, "All right, so I fainted. I've never climbed up a cliff before, and I thought I'd lose my hold of your sister, and she would have fallen to the bottom. It wasn't a pretty thought — do you realize what would have happened to her?"

Timmy said, with a sob, "She would be deaded."

His brother turned on him in fury. "Shut up, Timmy!" so he stopped crying and stared at me. He was so dirty, and so were the others. "What is more to the point, are you going to tell *him*?" the big boy demanded of me.

"Him? You mean Mr Stanton?" I thought about it. "I doubt it. He told me to come out and see that none of you did anything dangerous. I daresay he wouldn't be above giving you a whacking — all three of you!"

The little girl said, "You mean you won't tell?"

"That's right," I said cheerfully. "I'm feeling better now. We can talk. What made you all get in such an idiot situation?"

"We were exploring," the big boy said impatiently. "You really mean you won't tell *him* what happened? No strings?"

I thought about it. For their own safety, there must be strings. I said so. "I'm supposed to be in charge of you three, part of the time. Now, if I don't tell Mr Stanton about this escapade, then you three have to stop playing those stupid dangerous practical jokes on me. Clear?"

They looked at each other. "Oh, those!" the big boy said in fine scorn, "that was just to test you. Did you tell anyone?"

"About the broken steps, yes. About Cotton Dodgers, no. But let's have this plain, all three of you. This is my holiday, as well as work. I'm going to hospital to learn to be a nurse, when the summer holidays are over, and I'm not going to have my holiday spoilt. I'm an orphan, and I have to look after myself. And that's what I'm going to do," I said, thinking a tough line might work well with them.

It did. "An orphan? That's funny, so are we!" the little girl said. "My name's Jenneth Holbrook, and this is my brother Sheldon, and Timmy's younger than me."

"Shut up, Jen, I'll talk," Sheldon said. "We don't want a governess or a nursemaid."

He couldn't have been more than ten, I thought. He had a gallant tilt to his chin. He had, so far, been in charge of the other two, and after all, ten is no age to realize that you're alone in the world.

"But you'd like *some*one, wouldn't you?" I asked him, softly. "I don't really rank with the grown-ups. When I go to hospital, I shall be about the youngest there, and I'll be bossed about by everyone. Why don't we four just team up, and have fun when they let me out?"

Sheldon was still suspicious, but the others agreed. Then Sheldon said suddenly, "If you're going to be a nurse, hadn't you better do something about your hands? They look a mess, and they might get germs in those cuts."

Next day I was able to go to the village, and I took the children with me. They all wore the same shabby shorts and shirts, but I had got at them and mended the

50

tears, and the children's faces and hands were clean, their hair neat, to start out with, at least.

They said. "We won't come in the shop with you. They don't like us in there. We'll stay outside."

"No. You come inside with me, or I'll tell on you. I don't trust you — how can I? Remember Cotton Dodgers?"

For some reason it quelled them and they agreed to go inside with me.

The postmistress screamed at the sight of them, but I said quietly, "It's all right. They'll be good. They're with me," and I gave them some small change to buy sweets with while I telephoned the hospital.

Nolan Pearce wasn't as badly injured as I had feared, and they let him have a telephone table. "Are you all right, Emma?" his voice came over the wire. "I've been so worried. What happened to you?"

"I got taken in an ambulance to another hospital. I'm all right," I said. "How long will you be laid up?"

"Not all that long. This bed's wanted," he told me cheerfully. "I'll have this leg in plaster and be able to hobble about.

Emma, when I'm about again, I'd like to come over and see you. Would it be allowed?" he asked.

"I don't know, but I expect we could meet here in King's Dassett, if you liked," I told him.

I didn't have long to talk, and when I put the receiver down, bought my cotton and ushered the children out, they asked me who that was.

"It's a doctor I met on the train coming here," I told them.

"Does Mr Stanton know about him?" Jenneth asked.

She had a cute little face when she wasn't looking deadpan. I said, "No, why should he? It isn't anyone else's business."

"We won't tell," Sheldon said fiercely, as if he thought I suspected him of reporting me.

"It's just a friendship," I said. "A person should have at least one friend."

"Ladies and gentlemen don't be friends," Jenneth said pertly. "They get married."

"Who told you that?" I smiled. "It's different with doctors and nurses, anyway. We talked about hospitals and injured people and medicine and things like that."

"Well, that's better than old history," Sheldon growled. "Who does he think he's fooling?"

"Who?" I asked, startled. We were walking back over the causeway. The children seemed to be quite sure of themselves, regarding tide times. They had no fears.

"Heywood Stanton, of course," Sheldon and Jenneth said together. "You know, of course, what his name means? Heywood means 'out of the dark forest' and Stanton means 'from a stony place'. He's horrible, like his names."

I couldn't help reflecting that his names suited him. "Still, he has you children there for the holidays, and I'm sure I don't know why he should, because you were very tiresome on the day I arrived. Heaven knows what tricks you got up to before then," I said severely. "Besides, names don't really matter."

"Yes, they do. We heard you say your name was Emma and anyone knows that means 'one who heals' and you're going to be a nurse. So there you are. That proves it!" Jenneth said in some triumph.

They were a taking bunch of children, when I got to know them better. Heaven knew what sort of upbringing they had had, but they were enterprising and not without knowledge. I found myself liking them more every day; most of all, I think, that appealed to me about them, was their courage. Timmy occasionally gave a strangled sob in moments of tension, but he was such a little boy, and even he dried up and was instantly quelled by a look from his elder brother.

They wanted to show me the cave of the island's pirate, but it was out of bounds. They tried three times to enveigle me over there, but each time someone guessed their intentions and stopped them. So in disgust they left it to another time.

Compromise in the shape of a picnic on the beach facing the mainland was resorted to. It was a blistering hot day. I had not seen Heywood Stanton since the day before, but I had helped in the kitchen, assisted Mrs Boyd with her mending and chatted with her about my future career; I had painted a cupboard in the kitchen for Mrs Abbott and done my room out. Now I was free for the afternoon provided I kept the children with me. We were starting off when Heywood Stanton appeared and called us back.

The children shrank back against a wall with creeper growing on it, as if they expected him to chastise them. They all looked so guilty. I said crisply, "Did you want us, Mr Stanton? We're only going to the South Beach for a picnic."

"Come into the house for a moment. There's something I want to say to you," he snapped.

I followed him back, leaving the picnic basket with the children. I found he had retreated to the study. I followed him in, and he stood there, tall, morose, looking down at me with no great pleasure, those light eyes of his boring into mine.

"Has my mother told you about the children?" he asked.

"Yes, Mr Stanton. At least, she told me they are orphans and that they lost their father in a tragic way, if that's what you're referring to."

He flinched a little. "Did she say how?" he asked, in a low tone.

"No, and I didn't like to ask. But she did warn me that the children didn't know.

She said they thought he had just got ill and died."

"And did she tell you to watch the children at all times and don't let them go near the top floor of the house?" he continued.

"She gave me to understand that it is part of my job to keep them in sight and out of mischief. But as I'm allowed to go to the sewing-room, and I usually sew for them, why can't they be with me there?"

He looked startled for the moment, then he said, "I wasn't talking about the sewing-room, but in view of their enterprising habits, it might be as well if the children went no farther up than their own rooms. And don't listen to the wild tales they tell you. Use your own sense, and if in doubt, ask Mary Abbott or her father."

I promised I would, and I started to escape, but he suddenly called me back, sharply. "What happened to your hands?" he asked, and he came to me and took my hands in his.

I've met a lot of young men in my short life; young uncles and brothers and cousins of school friends, and I have had my hands taken in a man's before now, and thought little of it. But his hands holding mine had the most peculiar effect on me. I was so startled that I couldn't think what to say. I tried to tug them away but he held my hands fast, and I winced.

"Sorry, didn't mean to hurt you," he said. "Keep still. How did you get these deep scratches and tears?"

I just wanted to escape from him, so I said anything, to terminate this conversation. "I was idiot enough to try to climb some rocks but it was all right. It gave me a chance to try nursing on myself," I jabbered.

"What rocks? Where?" he insisted.

"I don't know. I don't know the island well enough to explain and honestly, it doesn't matter, does it? Please let me go, Mr Stanton. The children might escape and then I shan't know where to look for them."

It was an inspiration. He let me go at once, because he, too, was always anxious about their whereabouts. But as I ran out of the house shaking in every limb from that close touch of his hands on mine, I reflected that I wouldn't hear the last of that.

The children wanted to know what he had been on about all that time. I thought I had better tell them. "He saw my hands and wanted to know how I'd scratched them like it," I said.

We were hurrying down towards the South Beach as I said it. They stopped. "You didn't tell on us?" Jenneth cried indignantly.

"No, I said I had been climbing rocks, but I don't think he believed me. You must trust me. I told you I wouldn't tell on you."

Sheldon put down the picnic basket and began ripping off his shorts and shirt. He had ancient swim trunks underneath. "Of course she won't tell on us!" he said scornfully to his sister. "Can't you tell? She's like us."

"Oh! Yes, she is, isn't she?" Jenneth said, considering me, and then pulling off her top things to follow her brother into the water.

I watched them. Timmy didn't even stop to peel his tops off. He just ran in as he was, laughing and shouting. He had no formal swimming strokes like Sheldon. As with Jenneth he got about in the water, easily, eel-like. They all loved the water. No need to worry about these children. And come to think of it, if I hadn't come along when they were stranded on the cliff-face, I daresay they would have got out of it themselves, somehow. Jenneth would have managed to get her shoe off in time and escape. Then why did everyone worry about them so much?

When the children came out, I dried them off roughly, and left them to run about and finish drying. Timmy, as always, was hungry. Mary Abbott's cooking was plain and wholesome. Enormous filled sandwiches, hunks of plain fruit cake, gingerbread, even cold bread pudding, and the children stuffed until they fell asleep.

I sat back watching them, as one by one they stopped eating, and stretched out on the old blanket I had brought down with me for the purpose. Like their hard play, they slept deeply. They did everything with vigour and an exaggerated thoroughness. Did they remember much of their father, I wondered? I had seen no sign of grief so far, yet it had apparently been recent, his death. I wondered how it could have happened and concluded that it might have been a train or road accident.

And then, left to myself, I inevitably came back to thinking of Heywood Stanton, and the effect of his holding my hands. I shivered, yet the excitement was not unpleasant. I just didn't understand it. With one part of me I wanted to leave the island at once, and with the other part of me, I wanted to stay. Perhaps tomorrow, tonight even, he might demand my services, typing those notes of his on Roman times, and how would I feel then, going into that study of his, looking up into his dark face with those keen light eyes boring into mine? How could I sit down and calmly type about Roman remains, when here was pulsating life coursing through my veins so that I hardly knew how to hold my pencil?

The sun momentarily blotted out by a cloud, I shivered, but it wasn't so much at the little chill wind that had sprung up, but at the memory of what I had overheard that first day, when he had been speaking to his mother, and he had mentioned 'the occupant of the top floor' being upset by my appearance in the house. And now he didn't want the children to go to the top floor. What on earth could his secret be, that he couldn't have the children go near, yet his mother was so much in need of female company owing to the isolation imposed by that secret, that she had been forced to seek a companion, even if it was only myself, just out of school, and only here for a brief eight weeks?

My heart beat uncomfortably fast, and I looked up at Moon House with something like real fear. From this angle on the beach, the house, perched on a rock, looked rather like a small fortress. There were only two windows in that whole end wall, looking out on to this particular beach, and I couldn't tell whether they were on the first or second floors. Which was the controversial 'top floor' where that occupant was, who must be considered when it came to a strange young female being admitted to the house for any length of time. Into my mind flashed the thought of a man, a man to be scared of, a man who would scare me more than Heywood Stanton did. But then, my confused thoughts clamoured, did Heywood Stanton really scare me?

2

THE days settled into a pattern. The children knew I could only give them part of the afternoon for fun, so they had a temporary truce and kept within bounds in the morning, and out of mischief.

"You've done wonders with them," Mrs Boyd told me, as I took away a sheaf of letters to type for her. "Life is peaceful here at last!"

I had to type in the study, when it was empty. I never knew where Heywood went in that hour allotted to me for his mother's letters. He just seemed to vanish.

His mother wrote the most intriguing letters. Those to the person called 'Darrell' were guarded in the extreme but appeared to me to be begging the person to do what she wanted. The letters to other people — friends abroad and relatives — were chatty, garrulous, even, but didn't really say anything, at least, not about herself. It was mainly answering theirs.

She told me once that if you didn't write long letters to people, you couldn't expect to get any back. She got many back. The postman came out every day from King's Dassett with them. She seemed to be trying to convince herself that she wasn't living a lonely existence on an island with a son who was a recluse.

If I had ever wondered about that word before, I didn't now. He worked in his study; he vanished. We didn't see him at meal-times, and it was I who played cards or sat talking and sewing with his mother in the evening. The rooms, with their stone walls, were always chilly, and she talked mainly about the time when she lived in the warm parts of the earth. She never mentioned the thought of returning to them. She seemed to think she would have to stay at Moon Island for ever.

"Why is it called Moon Island?" I asked her idly one night.

"Why, because of its shape. It's like a crescent moon," she said. "We did have a map of it somewhere. You must find it, to help you get about. Ask my son for it, next time you work with him."

That was the next day. He had masses

of stuff he wanted typed; so much that he asked his mother to let me off working for her that day. He said curtly that he was getting behind. I thought she was going to make a retort, perhaps about it being his own fault for neglecting the study so much. But he looked at her, hard, and she didn't speak.

I went into that room with as much excitement racing through me as I knew I should, and I went to terrific lengths to prevent his fingers touching mine when I passed him papers of typescript.

I forgot to ask him for the map after all. I found him looking at my hands. "I see they've healed," he remarked. "Let that be a lesson to you, not to go climbing rocks again. Besides, it wouldn't do for the children to know you had such tastes. Hard enough to keep them out of mischief as it is."

"They're very reliable children," I said. "Did you know how well they can swim?" and I fancied he looked surprised. "Don't you ever go swimming with them?"

"I have rather too much to do to go swimming with anybody," he said rather curtly. But almost at once, he looked as if he was sorry he had said that. "Unless you want to be taken swimming. Do you?"

"You mean I can't go swimming unless someone is with me?" I was puzzled. I hardly thought he meant he would like to go with me. "The coast isn't all that dangerous, is it?"

"No, and I didn't mean that," he said. "If you would like me to go swimming with you, then I will. Is that what you meant?"

That man really liked putting me on the wrong foot. I went pink and stammered, "I wasn't angling for — I mean, I wouldn't want to take you away from your work — well, I mean, if you'd take the children. They'd love it."

"I doubt that," he said dryly. "But I will go swimming with you, tomorrow morning, since you appear to want it and are too embarrassed to ask."

Did I want it? Honestly, I didn't know, but it did seem unfair of him to make it seem that I had. I miserably finished my notes. There was a lot of work. I had to refer to him for the spelling occasionally, and to dates to which he made reference, to be looked up. He said suddenly, "You're really interested in this, aren't you?"

I caught a glimpse of my face in the glass doors of a book case. I was all aglow like an idiot, because I did really care a lot about the work. I loved it, in fact. All I could do was to nod at him.

He managed to look pleased without actually smiling. "It's the one thing I have," he said, softly, and then looked angry at such an admission.

That was the pattern of things. If we came near to an understanding, he usually managed to seem angry about something before I left the room. I didn't understand him. I was glad to get back to the uncomplicated companionship of the children who, having decided not to plague me any more, were the perfect companions.

The day following that, Heywood Stanton was as good as his word, and went swimming with me. He might, of course, have warned me that he intended to bang on my door at five-thirty in the morning. As it was, I fell out of bed, and in response to his curt demand for no time to be wasted, I fell into my swimsuit and towelling wrap, and rushed down, pulling on a rubber cap as I went, hardly with the sleep out of my eyes. He looked down at me and grinned.

"You look sleepy. Can I trust you not to get into difficulties?" And that, of course, was calculated to sting me awake, and it did.

He was a business-like swimmer. No dallying in the water for him. He said we would swim out to a red marker buoy we could see, and without asking me if I could swim that far, he was off. I had all I could do to keep up with him. But I did. Temper wouldn't permit me to let him beat me. He seemed surprised. He stood, a splendid brown figure, briskly towelling his back on the beach, looking down at me getting a stone out of my shoe.

"Stand up. I'll do it," he ordered, and when I said I didn't want him to, of course, he insisted, and there was that fierce stupid excitement running through me, as he held my foot cradled in his hand, and examined the scratch from the flinty stone. "You're a baby — you just don't take care. Look at that! Or is it that you want to make opportunities for practising that nursing skill you're hoping to acquire?"

I wriggled free from him and mumbled

that it was an accident.

"Want to swim tomorrow?" he demanded.

I did but I dare not. I said I'd think about it, but that didn't please him. He grunted, and strode off back to the house, leaving me with a throat aching with unshed tears. Why hadn't I said I had wanted it badly? Of course I wanted to be with him, as much as possible!

It was then that I happened to look up, right up to the very top of the house, to the parapet that hid most of the roof, and I thought I saw a movement up there. The children? Oh, no! With my heart in my mouth, I hurried into the house to find out where they were, but they were already dressed, skirmishing downstairs in search of food.

"You've been swimming!" they accused. "Why didn't you take us?"

"I didn't think you'd be awake," I said, finding the first excuse possible. "Listen, I just thought I saw someone move on the top of the house. Now tell me honestly, was it any of you? The truth, now!"

They gaped at me. "You don't mean that," Sheldon said at last. "I mean, you don't think we'd go up there, after you said *he* said we weren't to be even allowed as high as the sewing-room?"

"Well, I didn't think you would," I said lamely, "but who could it be?"

"Don't you know? Honestly?" little Timmy said, leaning hard against me, and playing with the sash of my towelling wrap.

"No, I don't. Am I supposed to?"

They considered it, and seemed about to say something, when the most tempting smell of kippers came up the staircase. They whooped and shot past me, hungry as always. There was no hope of asking them then. "Tell you at breakfast!" Jenneth shouted.

Mrs Boyd would be surprised, I thought, when she heard that her son had been swimming with me. I can't think why he did suggest it. Usually he was frosty with me, rather than friendly.

She must have forgotten what I told her about overhearing her conversation, because when I went along to the bathroom, I heard them talking again.

Heywood was saying, "Well, I've had trouble with her. I didn't expect it and I hope it won't happen again."

What trouble, I thought? Surely he isn't going to tell his mother I had refused his invitation to swim again?

She said, "Well, why did you swim where she could see you?"

"How did I know she'd get up so early? I wish you'd go up and soothe her down. Hysterics at this hour of the morning is not to my taste."

"It's no use asking me to go, Heywood. She doesn't even like me. You'll have to be a little more careful if you don't want her to see you with Emma. You might have known how it would be."

"Yes, I might have known," I heard him say bitterly.

What was all that about, for goodness' sake? I remembered the remark of the 'occupant of the top floor', on the first morning I was here, and suddenly it dawned on me that the floor on which the sewing-room was, was not really the top floor. There must be one above it.

And according to that piece of overheard conversation, I thought, with hot cheeks and miserable shame, it must be a woman up there. A woman prone to hysterics. It was also possible that that was where

Heywood went when the study was empty and free for me to type his mother's letters. And the woman didn't like to see Heywood with me.

Slowly it crept into my mind that that was his wife up there. That might excuse his manner to me. If he were married, of course he would not be free to be friendly with me. But he had gone swimming with me, and he could raise a terrifying pitch of excitement in me by just touching me . . .

I wished I had someone to talk to about this. Someone older than I was. Some aunt or grandmother. An outsider who could see things clearly, and who didn't know the family.

I got through my routine jobs as quickly as I could and went in search of the children, to ask them about what they had said on the stairs that morning, but they were in a tricky mood, and kept laughing and avoiding me, determined for some reason, not to answer my questions.

They didn't want me to explore the island, either. "You promised me you'd buy ice-cream at King's Dassett," Jenneth shouted, and Timmy wanted chewing gum.

Sheldon just looked reproachful.

"And what am I supposed to have promised you?" I asked him.

He shrugged. "It doesn't matter. But I did want to get a film for my camera, and it is just over the causeway and we would have time before high tide."

I supposed that the shop had more attractions for them than the island, which they knew like the back of their hands. I made a bargain. "If I take you over the causeway and wait while you buy what you want, will you take me exploring the island?"

They exchanged that secret glance, and whispered together. "All right, tomorrow, but not today," they said. "You went swimming today, with Heywood Stanton, and you didn't take us."

I was careful to ask Mrs Boyd if I could take them to the mainland. She looked at me rather oddly, I thought. "You can take them farther, if you like. There's a bus that runs into Chighampton. Why not take a sandwich lunch?"

I couldn't believe my ears. She said, with a faint smile, "Well, you are not a prisoner on Moon Island, you know. You only have to ask, if you want to go farther and you've done everything you're required to do by way of little jobs. And provided you keep the children with you, of course."

The children. Yes, I saw that I was really there to keep them out of the adults' way. They were an encumbrance, poor brats. I said warmly, "I'll be glad to take them and I'm sure they'll love it. What time must I bring them back?"

"Don't worry about the tides — you can always get a boat — but I would prefer you to get them back by six. They're such a nuisance to get to bed if they get tired — well, the two younger ones, that is."

There was the question of what the children should wear. She looked embarrassed. "Well, Chighampton is not very smart, and their clothes are all right for the beach if they're clean, surely?"

I put the children into their least worn shorts and shirts, and made some sandwiches myself. Mary Abbott looked alarmed for the moment, in case she should be expected to stop what she was doing, and take on the job. When I told her she wasn't to bother, she was frankly suspicious.

"You're a willing lass," she said. "Too willing. What are you hoping to get out of this?"

"Out of what?" I asked sharply, reddening. I didn't like her tone.

She wrung out the cloth in the bucket and wiped down the section of flagged floor she had been cleaning on her knees. "This job. It's just drudgery, the things they expect you to do, and it being your school holiday and all. And you so willing, you'd take the jobs from other people. Is it that you fear being idle? Or are you sucking up to *them?* There's no money there, I can tell you, not after what happened."

I laid down the bread knife. "What *did* happen?"

"I've said too much," she scolded herself. "That's me all over. Can't keep my mouth shut. All I will say was that before it happened there was money and plenty. Now there's not, and he gets more turned in on himself every day and him not yet out of his early thirties. It's not right."

I couldn't get any more out of her than that. I did say coldly, "I like people, and I like to be busy and I'm not hoping to get more than a roof over my head and enough to eat, until I go to the hospital to train," but she was sceptical. Later, I learned why, but at the time, I just thought she was a disgruntled person, tied to the island and to drudgery in the big house.

The children were thrilled with the thought of a day out. "Keep quiet, for goodness sake, in case anyone changes their minds and stops us," I warned them. I meant Heywood Stanton. I was quite sure he wouldn't approve of the idea. But we got off the island without being stopped, and Mary Abbott — as if sorry she had been so bitter — had at the last minute put in a jam turnover for each of us, and an apple and banana each. "If you're buying drinks, make it good wholesome milk, not this fizzy stuff. It makes them sick," she said tartly.

I telephoned Dr Pearce at the hospital. He was making strides, and looking forward to seeing me again. "Where are you bound for today, Emma?"

I told him. Nostalgia was in his voice. "Chighampton! Oh, if only I hadn't had this rotten bit of luck and got bogged down in hospital."

"Never mind, you'll soon be out at this rate," I told him.

"Don't ring off!" he shouted suddenly, as I was about to put the receiver down. "I've just remembered. Don't let the children go to the north end of Chighampton. They're excavating there. Dangerous."

I promised I wouldn't, and wondered why he thought they would want to, if it was as popular a seaside resort as I had heard. I said goodbye and went to find the children.

Sheldon said, "Is it your fiancé you keep telephoning?"

"No, it's just that doctor I met in the train accident on the way here." I saw no reason to keep it a secret. "He's going to work in Chighampton, and he wanted to visit the island."

"They won't let him, you know. No strangers allowed there," Sheldon said.

"Oh, of course they will! *I* was a stranger, wasn't I?" I laughed.

"You're different. You were going to work there. It's visitors and reporters they don't like. They think every visitor is a reporter in disguise."

"Good gracious, what for? Why should

newspapers be interested in Moon Island?" I said, shepherding them to the bus stop.

"Because of the secret," Jenneth put in importantly.

The secret. The one which I had heard Heywood and his mother discussing? Oh, no, that must just be something personal he was keeping quiet. I said, "Now what secret do you think there is at Moon House?"

"It's a witch they keep locked up on the roof," Timmy said, with ghoulish satisfaction.

"Well, it's a *Thing*, anyway," Jenneth corrected him. "I don't know what it is, but it's a *Thing*."

"Now that I won't believe and you are not to say such things. It's a lady, isn't it? Someone who isn't very well. Mr Stanton goes up to see her."

"Did he tell you that?" Jenneth asked, in awe.

"No, he didn't. I pieced it together from what other people have said," I told them hastily. I couldn't let these children know I had eavesdropped, however accidentally that eavesdropping had been.

"Well, it's mysterious enough to make some chap come every so often and watch the house through binoculars," Sheldon said, with his best grown-up voice. "You can see the sun glinting on them. It's always a give-away."

"Sheldon, really!" I laughed at him. "Just how old are you, I'd like to know? Ten?"

It was what I honestly thought, but it brought a howl of derision from the children, not unmixed with indignation. "Our Sheldon's twelve, going on for thirteen," Jenneth exploded.

"And Jen's nine, rising ten, in case you're going to say she's a kid of six," Sheldon said.

"Oh, I apologize all round," I told them gravely. "But no one told me, and you must admit that the tricks you played on me when I first arrived, weren't the work of older people like you, Sheldon." And he reddened.

"Well, we didn't know what you were like and we didn't want a nursemaid. If we'd known you were a sport, we wouldn't have done it," he growled.

We settled on the bus, determined to have a good day. I thought about Nolan Pearce and that promising friendship that he appeared to be offering me. He was nice. No sudden moods, no mysteries about him. And that brought me, inevitably, to Heywood Stanton.

I turned to Sheldon. "How long have you known Mr Stanton?"

He glanced quickly at me. "Oh, years and years," he said. "At least, he used to come to our house, though we were away at school. He was our father's friend."

That astonished me. I twisted round to look at him. He was behind me, the two young ones were sharing my double seat and sprawling all over me.

"You mean that Heywood Stanton was your father's friend? *Really*?"

"Yes. But I don't think he was so ratty then. Letters from home didn't give me that feeling. I mean, he came to stay sometimes, and they played cards and golf and all that. Mrs Boyd came too. And a cousin of theirs."

"But I thought you three were strangers to them!"

"Well, we were, weren't we?" Sheldon said logically. "I mean, we were at school — even Timmy — and in the hols we usually went to our grandmother's in Scotland. That was fun, only she's dead now so we can't go."

"What did your father do, that he should be friends with Mr Stanton? The same thing — writing?"

"Oh, no," Sheldon said with heavy patience, "our father was a pathologist. At a hospital. In London."

"*Was* he? Holbrook? I never heard of him but then I suppose I wouldn't!"

"He wasn't famous," Sheldon said fairly. "But well known, I think."

Then, I thought, he should have left enough money for these children to be dressed decently, and a wave of anger went over me. I would buy them some decent clothes while we were out today, and have them charged. Surely that would be possible? It wasn't fair. How could I take them out like this?

The sun came out suddenly and cheered us all up, and it grew hot. The little ones got over-excited and out of hand. I was glad when we arrived. I found a quietish place on the beach for our picnic and they were all right when they were swimming, and playing ball games on the sand. But after we had demolished all the food, that was going to be the difficult time.

We found a fun fair and I spent all the spare cash I had on me, excepting the bus fares, and after that I suggested going to the shops and finding them new shorts and shirts, and a pretty dress for Jenneth.

Quite surprisingly, they thought it was a poor idea. They didn't want new clothes. And in that store, I lost them.

Somehow they had found it necessary to go back on their word and play games. Had I let them get bored? I didn't know. I spent a very heated time finding first one and then the other. At last I collected all three.

I said to Sheldon, "That was mean. If you didn't want to stay in the Store, why didn't you say so, in a civilized way? I'm not all that much older than you are, and you might be decent and not worry me when I've got the responsibility of the three of you."

Chastened, they went with me back to the beach. I thought I'd give them another couple of hours and then call it a day. This end of the town was where the cliffs were. I didn't know there were caves. It looked a nice part, and I thought it might take their minds off getting bored. Hotels of the quiet family type were above the cliffs, and there was a long slope and a lift, both for prams and wheel-chairs.

Sheldon growled, "The old fuddy-duddies come here."

"Let's go to the other end again," I suggested, but the children wouldn't. So we walked along the edge of the water, and that pleased them. With shoes round our necks, we all paddled, and eased out after the last altercation. Where were the good companions I had had on the island? Did Chighampton have this adverse effect on the children? If so, I wouldn't bring them here again, I decided. And at that point, I realized that Jen and Timmy were no longer paddling behind me. They had slipped away again.

"Sheldon, help me find them!" I said, exasperated, "and then we'll go home! I don't think I've enjoyed this day much."

"It's because of Aurelia," he said with a shrug. I stopped dead in my tracks. "Because of *what*?"

"Aurelia. The girl on the roof," he said patiently. "We don't like not to be believed and you thought we were spinning you yarns."

"But did you expect me to believe that there was a witch or a *Thing*?"

"Oh, that! That's just Timmy's way of saying she's so pretty and so peculiar. He's frightened of her. He's never seen anything like her."

"But I don't believe it! Keep someone a prisoner on the roof! It's ridiculous to expect me to believe that."

Sheldon kicked stones ahead of him as he walked. "She's not *out* on the roof," he explained patiently. "She's got living quarters built into the roof, and there's a flat between the humps of roof and they've made a roof garden for her to sunbathe. That's what the Peeping Tom looks at through binoculars."

I stopped dead in my tracks. "You really mean there's someone very beautiful and young up there? All alone? Why?"

"Oh, no, not alone. There's someone to look after her. And Mr Stanton goes up a lot. I don't know why she's there. I just know she's there."

"Pretty and peculiar? How is she peculiar?" I persisted.

He looked distinctly uncomfortable. "Well, she is. If you go near her, she says dotty things, and she's always dressing up, out of a box."

I didn't know whether to believe him or not. If I could believe it, it did rather make more sense of the fact that whoever was up there didn't like Heywood going swimming with me. But then there had been that other odd reference to this person, whoever she was, when Mrs Boyd and Heywood had been saying that "the occupant of the top floor" might go into a passion about my arrival, or words to that effect. "How long has she been there?" I asked the boy. I had forgotten the children, I was so shocked.

He was starting to tell me, when Jen and Timmy came flying towards us, looking scared and both talking at once. "Come quickly. There's someone being queer, choking. Do come!"

I ran with them, up from the beach to the promenade. This end of the promenade was almost unfinished, and far from the family hotels and in fact, far from everywhere. There was nothing but rough grass and bushes and the crumbling end of the unfinished breadth of cement, that was to have been a very smart built-up area.

A lonely invalid chair was in the middle of the expanse, and an elderly man was humped in it, gasping for breath.

I rushed to him. He looked blue. I had seen something like this before. "We told him you were a nurse, Emma!" Jenneth shrilled.

The man forced himself to look up at me as I bent over him, and he made a feeble attempt to point to a pocket of his old-fashioned waistcoat. "Pills" I thought he said.

I slid a gentle pair of fingers in the pocket and found a tube of pills. "Cardiac," I murmured. "How many?" I asked him.

He put up one finger, and I shook a pill out and gave it to him. "Have we any water left, Sheldon?" I asked quietly. He gave me the bottle with the last drop. I put it to the man's lips.

We stood there watching him recover. The children said, "Why, he's getting better! Was it a magic pill?"

He smiled. He must have been about sixty, and handsome in his youth. Now he straightened up in his mechanical chair, and his colour gradually became normal. "Yes, it's a magic pill," he agreed, and smiled up at me. "So you're a nurse, my dear."

"Not yet. I've been a cadet, and I'm going to train, at St John's," I told him, and I suppose my voice must have sang with happiness at the thought, because suddenly the world of hospital seemed a safe happy place compared with my present position.

"And where are you all staying now? Are these your brothers and sister?"

The children said, "No, we're not. We wish we were. We live on Moon Island."

I almost missed the flattery of being desired as a big sister, in watching the startled look in his face as Moon Island was mentioned.

"Do you know it?" I asked him.

He said, thinking, "Do you know, I believe I would like these young people to go to my hotel with a message. I'm not sure I feel well enough to get myself back. I've come too far!" and he pulled out a notepad and wrote quickly on it. "Do you think they could find the Royal Hotel and give this in at the reception desk?"

They were thrilled to go, of course, but as they went, he said, "I didn't want to say what I have to in front of them. Who are they, and how do they come to be on Moon Island? As I remember it, Heywood Stanton had no children."

"You know him?" I whispered, and crouching down beside his chair I looked into his face, and I said, "They are the young Holbrooks. Mr Stanton has them in his care since their father died. His mother is there — Mrs Boyd. Do you know her?"

"Laura Boyd? Oh, yes, of course I do. But why have they got the Holbrook children in their care?"

"I don't really know, and I'm not sure I should be talking about it. Mrs Boyd told me that Mr Holbrook died in tragic circumstances, but the children just think he died of a normal illness, and she wants it to be left that way."

"Yes, she *would*!" he said, rather grimly, with a faintly malicious gleam in his eyes. "Who wouldn't? And what are you doing on the island, my dear, if you're going to train to be a nurse?"

"It's a holiday job, looking after the children, and odd jobs, because I've left my boarding school and I haven't any family or anyone." I looked round. The children weren't in sight yet. "I did so want to talk about this. I'm not sure I ought to stay on Moon Island. There's something very odd there. But the children need me. I wish I knew what to do."

"What do you *want* to do in your heart?" he asked me.

"Stay there, I suppose," I said, thinking of Heywood Stanton with a queer little thrill that was fear and pleasure mingled. I kept thinking of the fact that a pretty girl called Aurelia was in the roof apartment, and wondering how much about her the children had told the truth.

"I thought you did," the man in the wheel-chair said. "Look here, I'd like to hear more about this. Perhaps I can give some advice. My name is Ketwill, by the way, Colin Ketwill. I haven't much longer left to me, and I do like to be kept amused. I may be in a special position to advise you, too."

"How do you mean, Mr Ketwill?" I asked, catching sight of the children.

"Why, do you see, I used to own Moon Island."

3

WE had to run for it, across the causeway, and in our haste I forgot to warn the children not to mention what had happened that day.

Not that it mattered much that night, but at lunch next day the children blurted out about what we had done for the invalid in the wheel-chair.

"We think Emma's going to be a marvellous nurse," Jenneth told Mrs Boyd, "because he was all purple in the face and he couldn't breathe and he just pointed to his heart and Emma knew what he meant and gave him a pill and then he was all right and he said it was a magic pill."

"That's a rather garbled version," I murmured, as Mrs Boyd turned startled eyes on me. "It was an invalid from one of the hotels, having a heart attack. He showed me where to find his special pills. That's all."

"We saved his life," Sheldon said heavily. "If we hadn't been there, he would have died. They said so at the hotel."

"Then we saved his life," I said coolly. "It's all in the day's work. I shall be doing it every day at hospital and thinking nothing of it."

"How smug," Sheldon said, with an irritating grown-up air he had sometimes, copied, no doubt, from the big boys at his school.

Mrs Boyd said worriedly, "I don't think I like the idea of letting you all off the hook if this is the sort of thing that is going to happen to you. Perhaps you'd better not go to Chighampton again."

"Don't let's," Sheldon said. "I'd rather go to Poltoncross for a change."

"Mrs Boyd, I would like to get some clothes for the children. I'd like to take them to church on the mainland. I just want a little frock for Jenneth and some decent shorts and shirts for the boys."

"But they've got decent things. Haven't they told you?" she said.

The children all reddened. "Have you?" I asked them. I was so cross. They should have told me. I apologized to Mrs Boyd.

"I'm afraid you let them take advantage of you," she said. "Don't believe half what they say. Not a quarter even, not about anything. They are great spinners of yarns. They always have been, and Timmy is being trained by the other two. Such a pity, because they really don't know black from white now, when it comes to telling the truth."

I was shocked. I looked at them, and all three of them dropped their eyes, and then on the instant excused themselves and rushed out.

I did what she said. I discounted everything they had told me, with it the story of the beautiful girl on the roof who dressed up and was spied on by a peeping Tom on the mainland. It was probably a sick aunt or grandmother up there, who didn't like her male relative going swimming with a member of the staff like myself.

I felt better after that, about the roof story, but not so good about the children. *Now* where did I stand with them?

After a day out, there was an accumulation of notes to type for Heywood Stanton, but he didn't seem ready to work at once. Unlike his mother, he apparently didn't discount what the children said. He began,

"I overheard the children talking about you ringing up some doctor chap at a hospital. Is this true?"

I agreed that it was, and how I came to know him.

Heywood Stanton looked annoyed. "I would prefer it if you didn't communicate with other people while you are on the island."

"But he's my friend. You mean I can't contact my friends in my spare time?"

"If you telephone him, he'll want to come out to the island and we don't have strangers here."

"No, he won't want to come here! It's understood that I shall only meet him in Chighampton, which is where he's going to work when he's out of hospital. I don't suppose that will be until the holidays are over, anyway. He hurt his leg pretty badly, seeing to the injured in that train crash."

Heywood Stanton still didn't look happy about it. "I give you my word he won't come here, Mr Stanton," I urged. "But why should you feel like this? Do you think I would discuss your business with someone else?"

"Everybody discusses other people's

business," he snapped. "And I have a particular reason why I don't want mine discussed. Now let's get back to work, shall we?"

But he couldn't work. He was edgy and bad-tempered and nothing pleased him and I was near to tears of frustration at having my typing torn up and told to begin again.

At last he rang for some coffee, for both of us. "I'm sorry," he said. Suddenly contrite with a swiftness of change of mood which completely put me out of countenance. "I'm a boorish individual and not to be tolerated. Forgive?" And as I blindly nodded to that, he said, "We'll take a break. Now, how are you getting on with your other work?"

I said, "Muddling through," with a wry smile.

"Do you like my island?" he demanded, as if he really wanted to know.

"What I've seen of it, yes, but no one will show me over it, and I never seem to get time to get very far."

"I'll take you," he said suddenly. "There's a waterfall which is quite incredibly beautiful. And a clump of woodland with some very fine tree specimens. The old chap who owned the place before I did, put a lot of money into landscaping the place."

I said, my vagrant tongue running away with me in the pleasure of Heywood Stanton not being bad-tempered with me as usual, "Oh, yes, Colin Ketwill."

"You know him?" Heywood asked sharply.

I could have bitten my tongue out. "No, not really. We just met him yesterday, in Chighampton."

"Did you, indeed! And how much of our business did you tell him?"

"Mr Stanton, it wasn't like that at all!" I protested. "He was having a heart attack and I managed to get one of his special pills to him in time. Ask the children — they'll tell you!"

"They'd tell me anything," he said angrily. "The only time one believes the children, is if one happens to overhear what they are saying to each other. And what did you say to Mr Colin Ketwill?"

"I just waited with him while he sent the children back to the hotel for someone to come and fetch him. He asked where we were staying and if they were my brothers and sisters, and when I mentioned Moon Island, he just said in surprise that he had once owned it. That's all."

He looked broodingly at me. "I bought the island to hide away from everyone. I could have, too, only the people I have around me won't let me. My mother, the staff, and now you. I somehow thought you would respect my need to keep apart from the world."

"But what have I done? I just passed the time of day with a very sick man. I'm sorry, but I'm going to be a nurse and that's the only thing that matters to me. I like people. I like talking to them and helping them — all kinds of people. They're just people to me. I don't see why you should distrust me so. Or why you should want to cut yourself off from everyone."

"Why I want to is my business," he said heavily. He stared at me. "Do you *really* want to be a nurse?"

"Yes, I do. More than anything else," I said sincerely.

"Have you got any idea what life in hospital is like?" he said broodingly, and again I said I had.

"I don't believe you can have. You're too young. Well, all right, they might have let you go there to help out a bit, learn a bit of First Aid, see a bit of ward life. But what do you know of the tragedy that goes on behind the scenes? You only know of the people who come out cured. What do you know about those who don't?"

"I know some people don't survive, Mr Stanton," I said quietly. "I'd have to be very naïve if I didn't make allowances for that. Nobody likes the thought, but it's there. One has to accept it."

"That's only the half of it," he muttered. "What of the personalities behind the operations? What of the people behind the casualties who come in? What do you know of those who are so proud of their work, they can't allow they might make a mistake? What about the people who overwork, and go wrong without meaning to? What about the inefficient ones, who almost always cause a life to be lost sooner or later? The half-trained, the bunglers, the ones drawn on to the staff because they're so hard to get, and they're not much good when their services are procured?"

I didn't understand him or his bitterness.

"Well, Mr Stanton," I said reasonably, "come to that, what does a writer know about life in hospital?" I tried not to sound rude, but really, it wasn't his world, it was mine. And I had found out a lot about it.

He looked sharply at me, and took the point. "No, that's true," he said, and he closed his eyes and shook his head slightly, as if to clear his vision. "And if that's the life you want, I have no right to try and turn you against it. I do beg your pardon." And then he looked at me as if he was on the point of saying something else, and altered his mind.

He said he would take me over the island the next day, and meanwhile, after the coffee came, we got down to the work and got through it. And he thanked me when I got up to go. He had a really nice smile, although it vanished so quickly.

Meantime, there was this day to be got through, and Mary Abbott was already complaining about the children being tiresome. Mrs Boyd begged me to take them out somewhere, anywhere. "But try not to let people talk to you about my son and the island," she begged. "He has his right to his bit of privacy. It isn't any fun trying to work when there are so many distractions. And you know the rule — no strangers allowed here."

I nodded. Useless to argue, to tell them I didn't want to bring any of my friends over. Even Dr Pearce, I no longer wanted to come here, even if I could have got permission. As he was in the world of hospital, it would only start more friction.

I and the children went down to the little dinghy. They said they'd teach me to sail. It was a very small craft and they were very good at handling it. There was a rule that they must only sail round the island and not away from it. I wondered how soon that rule would be broken.

But there was trouble with the dinghy. "Someone's been at it," Sheldon said angrily. "It's that Macey boy. I'll kill him!"

I requested Sheldon not to talk like that. "I know it's only an angry remark but I'd rather you didn't."

"Angry remark! He's only a village kid. He's not supposed to touch our things. But they all do it. It's because we can't — " and he broke off furiously, his face so red that he looked as if it would burst.

Jenneth and Timmy stood watching him. "You nearly let the secret out," Jenneth remarked, with a coldly clinical interest.

I lost my patience. "Now look here, all three of you, what is this secret business? You're always hinting at it but people tell me not to believe what you say! Now I'm not so sure. You'd better tell me right away, or I shall have to go to Mrs Boyd about it."

They all three looked at me, and Jenneth remarked coolly, "Well, that won't get you anywhere, will it, because she's in it, too."

"But we can't go on like this," I exploded. "You *must* tell me what's going on! It's all tied up with not showing me round the island, isn't it?" It was a shot in the dark but it went wide of the mark. I fancied they looked relieved, and Sheldon, rapidly cooling down, said, "If you still want a conducted tour, we'll take you. But don't blame us, that's all."

Anything to keep him away from a boy called Macey who was reputed to have damaged the dinghy, I thought. I arranged with Mary Abbott's father, Oliver Cripley, to get the dinghy repaired. I was no sailor. I couldn't see what was wrong at all. It looked all right to me. But Oliver, after a critical look at it, remarked, "Ah, the Macey boy again. Well, kids is kids. They quarrel. There won't be no stopping this sort of hanky-panky till the kids all make it up."

"Why do they quarrel?" I asked him sharply.

"Well, it's because of this here — " he began, then suddenly he looked appalled and dropped his mouth open. Mary Abbott came up behind me. Silently. I hadn't heard her footsteps at all, but it was her time for coming away from the big house to get her father's mid-day meal. "*Father!*" she said warningly, and her father dried up like the children had.

"Oh, it's this secret again, I suppose," I said scathingly. "Well, I know how to get at the truth. I shall go to Mr Stanton himself."

"You do that, miss," Mary Abbott encouraged. "If so be Mr Stanton wants to tell you, then that's all right. It takes responsibility off our shoulders — it's not for us to say ought about it."

"Well, it's about time someone did," I said, and unwisely added, "I'm not at all sure the children know the truth, either, because Timmy is really frightened of what he calls the witch on the roof."

They looked honestly puzzled. There was no other word for it. "Don't listen to kids' tales, miss," Mary Abbott said at last. "I wasn't meaning that, anyway. What I was meaning was . . . well, it was about how the children's father died. They're not supposed to know, and quite rightly, I'd say."

I was astonished. It was the last thing I had thought of. "Well, if they don't know, what do they keep talking about a secret for?" I asked her.

"I expect they feel there is a secret, because the grown-ups keep breaking off their conversation when the children are about, but it's only because they talk a lot about how the poor gentleman died."

"How *did* he die?" I asked, still not understanding.

Mary went as red as a beetroot and her father stared at her, no doubt wondering how, after shutting him up, she had got herself into this corner. "I'm sure it's not for us to say, miss," she said primly, finally falling back on that hardy old remark of any well-trained servant.

I left it at that, and let the children take me on a conducted tour. I wondered, after we had started, if I should have told the grown-ups about it first. But the island wasn't all that large, I argued. It had the huge bay, facing seawards; fine white sand dotted with huge, picturesque rocks, backed by low cliffs on which grew dense vegetation. It was up this that we climbed, this ridge of reddish-brown rock, and pushed our way through the trees. Tangled, dank and cool, we hadn't pushed far inwards before the bright light of day was shut out, and it was all green and rustling and eerie and the children seemed unwilling to go too far.

"Well, where does this lead to and how far will it take us?" I asked. "And what are the hazards? You might as well tell me now!"

"There's squelchy boggy places," Timmy offered, "and we're not supposed to come here."

"Well, why bring me here?" I said in exasperation. "Come on, back to the beach and we'll go all round the island on foot."

"We can't," Jenneth said. "It's too deep, the water, I mean. In spots the sand doesn't get uncovered at all."

"Then we'll go back for the dinghy. It surely must be put right now," I said. "If we tack all round the island and keep putting inshore when there's something interesting to see — how would that be?"

Sheldon said he'd rather go to the mainland, Poltoncross for preference.

"What's at Poltoncross, for goodness' sake?" I asked him. The children all said together, "Pictures, ice-cream stalls, market stalls, lots of decent shops with toys and things for sailing — the lot."

"Really! And why didn't you say so the day we went to Chighampton?"

"Chighampton's biggest," Sheldon shrugged, "and the grown-ups said we were to go to Chighampton."

Just lately, I found that the children tended to develop deadlock arguments. I led the way back to the beach, collecting scratches as I went. We sat on the edge of the low cliff, dangling our legs over.

"Now look here," I said, "Don't let's spoil the summer holidays like this. What's wrong?"

Sheldon wasn't going to say. He had that mulish look on his face.

Jenneth and Timmy fidgeted. They were dying to speak, but I caught them exchanging that look with Sheldon, taking their cue from him.

"All right," I said, with resignation. "If it's going to be like that, it doesn't matter. It's all one to me. Quick with you, and we'll cross the causeway while we've got time and we'll go to Poltoncross, and woe betide any of you if you're still sulking when we come back."

They came to life at once. Quite clearly they didn't like being on the island. I remembered how they had looked the first time I had seen them, sitting with deadpan expressions on their faces, outside Mary Abbott's father's cottage. They had resented me, a stranger, and played bad tricks on me — or had they just been playing tricks on any newcomer, from sheer, sheer boredom? That was probably nearer the mark.

I got permission from Mrs Boyd to take

them, once I had made the explanation about the boat and the Macey boy. She seemed worried about that.

"The Macey boy!" she murmured, half to herself. "Oh, dear," she added.

"Can't you tell me what the significance is?" I pleaded. "How can I deal with the children if I don't know what's behind all this?" But she wouldn't explain. She said she would some other time. It was tiresome. Nobody would explain.

We got across the causeway, the children cheering up considerably, and we caught the bus to Poltoncross without mishap. Now I felt I could breathe again. The children settled down to play one of their complicated games, multiplying car numbers. They were all good at it. But my thoughts wandered. The bus went along the coast road, and for the first time I got a really good look at the island. It was larger than I had at first thought, and now I could see the flat in the middle of the two high roofs.

I said to the children, "Did you know that Mr Stanton is going to take me on a tour of the island tomorrow?"

They exchanged a very odd look. I had

expected, the minute I had said it, that they would clamour to come too, but they didn't.

"I suppose you've been all over it, you three?" I pursued, but they still didn't answer. "Oh, for goodness sake, don't you know it's rude not to answer?" I exploded.

Timmy said, "We're not supposed to answer that."

"Why not?" I asked, surprised.

Sheldon kicked his young brother, but for once Timmy didn't care. "It's because we were told not to explore, and we did. We didn't mean to. We were following that rotten George Macey."

"Good gracious, how can you three be so mean about a boy who hasn't had the advantages that you three have?"

Sheldon shifted irritably. "So would you, if you were us, Emma. It's the way he throws his weight about. He's new to the island. He said he was going to explore and he didn't care who tried to stop him, so we followed him to see he didn't do any mischief to our property."

"And did he?"

"No. He just snooped."

"Well, what is there to see that's so special?" I prodded.

Unwillingly, Sheldon said, "There's a waterfall. It's dangerous. The bridge across it is shaky."

"And of course it's necessary to go and stand on the bridge," I said caustically, getting an unwilling smile from them. "What else?"

"There's Black Valerian's Cave," Jenneth said excitedly. "He was a smuggler, hundreds of years ago. And you can get lost in the cave and never come out because it goes right down into the earth."

"And I suppose the Macey boy went in?"

"No, he's too chicken," Sheldon said with satisfaction. "Besides, it's railed off with a big wooden guard. You can't get in."

"Then how do you know about it?"

"We found it in an old guide book in the library at Poltoncross." It was Jenneth who said it and received a kick for her pains.

"Oh." I gasped. I thought I knew the reason for their wanting to go to Poltoncross today. There was no library in Chighampton.

Jenneth said, "No, we don't want to

go there today," which rather endorsed my fears.

But just as I was going to tell her pretty sharply not to expect to go there today, a man behind us leaned forward and said, with a strong Middle West accent, "Say, that sounds like a mighty interesting place you've found. Would it be that little old island beyond the causeway?"

We all froze him with a look, but I had to answer. I was in charge. This is what came of doing what Heywood didn't want us to — talking about his property in the hearing of other people.

"I'm sorry, but we're discussing private property," I said.

"Oh, I know one can't just go there. I did try to go over the causeway but the natives stopped me. There was the cutest village policeman said he'd have to telephone his sergeant if I didn't come off that causeway."

We all hated him for referring to the inhabitants of King's Dassett as the natives, and making such remarks about Mr Tellett, our local policeman. I said, "Yes, they are instructed to keep strangers away."

"Now why? Is the island haunted? I'd

sure love to take pictures of a real live ghost," the American said, and his voice was so loud that other people began to be interested. There was a young man who pricked up his ears and began to ask such searching questions about the island that I decided we'd better get off the bus. I didn't think. I said, "Come on, let's go!" and rang the bell. At least we got off the bus and it started up before the American realized we had escaped. But once the bus had gone, we all stood looking at each other. We were in deep country, just half way to Poltoncross. "*Now* what do we do?" Sheldon asked blankly, and looked at the little ones. Sheldon and I might have walked the rest of the way, but they would be tired out.

"I'm sorry, it was all my fault for starting on about it," I apologized to them. "But still, private property's private property. They've no right to keep on about it."

"It's not that," Sheldon said awkwardly. "It's something else."

"Oh, the secret, I suppose," I said sarcastically, and began to walk on.

"Yes, well, if you want to know, it is," he said fiercely. "We don't know what it was, but we heard someone talking about it once in King's Dassett. They were going on about it all being in the newspapers at the time."

"*What* was in the newspapers?" I exploded.

"We don't know, but we were living on the island so we said that it wasn't anyone else's business and that we'd tell Mr Stanton about them gossiping about him, so they shut up. But every time someone talks about Moon Island, someone remembers what was in the papers."

"When, Sheldon? When was it in the papers?" I asked gently.

"We don't know, but we think it was something to do with our father," he said, jerking his head away so that I couldn't see his face.

I would have given a lot to know which newspapers. Local or the national ones? If only we could have got into Poltoncross without incident! And just then, the answer to all our wishes drove up in the oldest and most majestic Rolls Royce I had ever seen. It was Colin Ketwill, our friend from Chighampton.

He told his chauffeur to slow down, and

leaned out of the back window. "Hello, young people, I was just thinking about you all. Where are you off to?" he asked, smiling.

Jenneth said bluntly, "Poltoncross, but we had to get off the bus because people heard us talking about the island and they wanted to go and see it. It was Emma's fault."

"Poor Emma," Mr Ketwill said, laughing. "I, too, was always in trouble with younger people. Get in, all of you, and we'll go to Poltoncross together because that is my destination."

"We're not supposed to thumb lifts," Jenneth said quickly.

"This isn't thumbing lifts, you clot," Sheldon hissed, and I said quickly, "This is perfectly all right, Jenneth, because we know Mr Ketwill and he's very nice. We would be grateful for a lift, sir," I said to him.

"Nicely said, my dear," and the old man began to open the door before his chauffeur could get out and come round.

Sheldon got the thrill of his life by being allowed to sit by the man. Jenneth and Timmy squeezed into the corner of the

111

far side of me so as not to discommode Mr Ketwill, and as we started off again, I asked him how his health was since we had seen him last.

"I've been splendid, my dear. Never felt better in my life. I expect it's through having made some young friends. I even played with the idea of contacting young Stanton and asking permission to take you all out for the day."

"But you didn't," I smiled. "You were afraid of us."

"I wasn't," he said stoutly. "Just couldn't make contact — the young blighter's had the telephone disconnected. He'll be sorry for that one day. I may be an old codger, but I recognize and bow before the necessity to have modern instruments of communication. We in this day and age are conditioned to use them. We can't do without them."

"What's he talking about?" Jenneth whispered.

"You can't do without the telephone, it's so useful," I translated.

"Oh. Yes, I wish we had the telephone, then we could ring up the Prime Minister and the headmaster of Sheldon's school (just for fun) and maybe the Queen."

"You are a clot," Sheldon said, from the front. "They have private numbers, not listed in the book — so people like you can't worry them."

Colin Ketwill smiled at them broadly. He was enjoying himself. "So refreshing," he kept saying. "So refreshing. Never been so entertained in my life. You'll all take tea with me, of course? I like chocolate eclairs and cream buns and ice-cream. None of your dry toast and tea cakes for me."

That went over well with the children. They voted him a good sort. He did us proud, too, in the most expensive hotel in the place. It had a balcony overlooking the beach, and after tea, the children were allowed to go down there and play while I stayed and talked to the old man.

"Well, my dear, what do you think of Heywood Stanton, eh?"

I couldn't stop my cheeks growing pink, but I answered civilly enough, "We don't always get on well, but after all, he's the boss. He seems to want to be pleasant but he seems weighed down with a heavy load of anxiety. He went swimming with me one morning, and he's promised me a tour of the island tomorrow. But he sometimes forgets to be pleasant and snaps."

"Yes," he said, "I'm not surprised. Most of us make mistakes, but most of us can shrug them off. Some people can't shrug off a mistake, or the effects of it, rather. It lives with them, to their life's end. I always say it's not the thing itself but the way the person handles it."

"I don't understand," I said.

He looked at me. "What would you say young Stanton does for a living?"

"He's a writer," I said promptly.

"At this moment, yes, possibly. But before. What would you think his career was?"

"I don't know," I said slowly, because at that moment all I could see Heywood Stanton in was a long white coat walking down a hospital ward, and that was silly. I didn't suppose he'd been in a hospital in his life, except to see his friend when he was dying. That, I imagined, was where he had picked up such a gloomy picture of hospital life, which he had painted for my benefit. "Other people apparently know," I said, "but nobody will tell me. Why?"

"Because nobody wants to be the one to do the telling, my dear. It's like Pandora's box. Once you've lifted the lid, you can't press it down again before the things inside escape."

"Well, the children keep on about a secret, and the stories they tell me are wild in the extreme and they connect them with the death of their father."

"H'm, tragic, that," he said.

"You knew about it, Mr Ketwill?"

"Well, yes, I knew them all at the time. The children were tucked away in their boarding schools, after the manner of certain Englishmen. Holbrook, of course, travelled a great deal, and after his wife died, he couldn't do with the children being at home. Pity he . . . died," he said, reflectively.

"What was he like?" I asked. Surely that couldn't hurt?

"A very nice man," Colin Ketwill said, without hesitation.

"Are the children like him?" I mused.

"No. The boys are like their mother. Jenneth, perhaps — well, her eyes are like her father's."

"How old was he? I mean, what age group?"

He smiled at me, thinking, no doubt,

that to anyone who was only eighteen, people above thirty were frankly old. He said, "He would have been nearing forty. Stanton, of course, is only, what? Thirty-two? Less, perhaps. That poor young man looks much older than he is."

"And he's lost his friend," I said. "The children told me he was their father's great friend."

"His best friend, I would say," Colin Ketwill said gravely. "Tell me, how does Stanton seem to you, my dear? Grief-stricken? Lost?"

"Angry," I said promptly. "He looks as if he would like to wipe young women of eighteen off the face of the earth sometimes. And at others, when we both get interested in his history — I'm pretty keen on Roman remains too, you see — then he seems to forget everything, and he tells me about life in Roman Britain, and he seems as if he's . . . escaped. Is that silly?"

"Far from it, my dear. Very near the truth, I would think. You know, if I were a young man again, I would want to spend a lot of time with you. You've got so much to give."

"*Have* I?" I thought he was being old-fashioned and courtly as by habit.

"You have indeed. Will you do me the honour of taking tea with me sometimes, and talking, just like this? It's a rare pleasure. Young women nowadays have lost the art of talking, it seems."

"Is it an art, Mr Ketwill?"

"It is, indeed. A lasting art. It outlasts looks, it overcomes the age barriers so that people of different generations can find a satisfying touching point. I don't feel old when I'm talking to you, my dear. I like it. Tell me, you still want to be a nurse?"

"Oh, yes, indeed I do!" I could hear the thrill and excitement mounting in my voice.

"Suppose you had so much money that you didn't have to work? Would you want to then?" he persisted.

"But of course! Anyway, I'd never have so much money."

"Ah, but who knows where wealth may fall from?" he smiled. "And Stanton, what does he feel about your leaving him to train as a nurse?"

"He loathes the idea, but then he would, wouldn't he?" I said.

He looked startled. "What do you mean by that?" he demanded.

"Well, he would, wouldn't he, because I seem to suit him as a typist and someone to talk to about Roman times, but he'll lose me when I go to hospital. That's what I meant."

"Oh, yes, well, of course. I see."

After that day, we met over tea on other occasions, and I felt he was an old friend. And the children had behaved very well, too.

He drove us back to King's Dassett, just in time for us to pelt over the causeway. He waved gravely from the back of the Rolls and was gone.

Next day was my tour of the island. I had looked forward to it very much. The children's dinghy was repaired, and they shoved off just before Heywood Stanton and I started out. I saw their little red sail go up as we plunged into the woods, and found the path.

Heywood Stanton was suitably dressed in jodhs and a khaki shirt, with a silk scarf tucked in at the throat. He wore dark glasses (I had noticed he wore them at all times when out of the house) and he didn't look the same man. He strode along, pointing out things, and I was near trotting to keep up with him.

Well, he had said the island was beautiful, and Colin Ketwill had said so too, but I must say that I felt the landscaping made it rather artificial. There was a chine running through the centre, made to look like a woodland idyll with a mountain stream, but when it was explained that it was only sea water pumped up, I thought it was a waste of money. The waterfall, seen from the bottom, was rather nice, until I heard from Heywood Stanton that it was a man-built pile of rocks, and a man-made fall of water, the same as the stream, it wasn't so attractive. I didn't see the purpose of it, either.

"Ketwill made over the island like this to bring home his bride, forty years ago," Heywood Stanton said shortly.

"Did she like it?" I asked, feeling that something was expected of me.

"She never saw it. She ran off with another man. He learned the hard way, never to trust a woman."

So that was it. Heywood Stanton was just a woman-hater. I supposed that some girl had walked out on him, too, at some time in the past. But something was required of me, so I said, "I think that's sad. He's such a nice man."

"How do you know? You've only met him once!" he said.

His eyes were boring into mine. I could have kicked myself. Blurt everything out, that's what I do. "We were given a lift by him yesterday and he took us to tea in Poltoncross," I said, with dignity.

"Given a lift?" he thundered. "How can I bring up those children to do the right thing if you encourage them to accept car lifts from a stranger?"

"He isn't a stranger, he's a sick old man, and I was with them and the chauffeur was driving. So it was all right."

"It wasn't all right and I forbid you to accept a lift again! What was wrong with the bus, anyway?"

Here I was, in for a penny, in for a pound. I said firmly, "We got off the bus because a strange American was speaking to us. We were half way there, and it seemed better to be picked up by someone who knows you so well, than to be bothered by a tourist who just wouldn't shut up."

"What was he pestering you for?" Heywood asked, looking ready to punch anyone on the nose who so much as looked at me.

"For the chance to visit Moon Island. He said he'd tried walking out on the causeway but the villagers had stopped them, and he called them natives. We hated him."

Heywood was livid then. His face was quite white with anger. "And I suppose you had all been talking at the top of your voices about the island?" he grated.

"No, I just asked the children what sort of places I should see when you showed me around today; it was something to talk about." I was smarting because it seemed so unfair. "Well, Mr Stanton, I would never have come here if I'd thought there was a secret that made it necessary for me to be guarded about the very place in which I was working. If you want to know, it makes me feel right-down peculiar when I go to the mainland."

"Does it indeed. It would apply with any job, anywhere, the need for discretion, in connection with your employer's affairs. And furthermore, with a temper like you've got, what makes you think you'd last five minutes in hospital?"

That was too much. "What makes you think you know so much about hospital life, Mr Stanton, when I have been in hospital and already worked there?" I stormed, stuttering in my fury.

There was an icy silence. "Yes, what indeed?" he said at last, on a low note.

The silence hung between us. Now was the time for apologizing again. I forced myself to. "I'm sorry. I won't take back what I said — I meant that. But I do apologize for saying it to you. I shouldn't have been so rude. I'm sorry about that."

To my surprise he laughed. "You bad-tempered brat," he chuckled. "Do you know your face is so red, it looks like a balloon about to explode?" He took my chin on the tip of one finger and tilted up my face. I wouldn't look at him at first and then I had to. "You certainly liven things up. And I should apologize, Emma. I'm always appearing to bait you, aren't I? It isn't that. I get bitter, and you're so young and fresh, you make me feel as old as the hills and as unhappy as — Ah, well," he said, letting me go. "Let's forget it, shall we, and call a truce? What do you say?"

I nodded, but I didn't want to shake on it. He had me. "You can't call a truce without a handshake," he objected.

So I had to, and he must have felt my hand trembling in his. I couldn't stop it. I was shaking all over. He looked at me, and then he remembered the scratches and cuts and examined both my hands. There was little to see now, but I made the mistake of trying to pull away from him.

"What's the matter? Do you find me so distasteful that you can't even bear to be touched by me?" he asked harshly.

"It isn't that," I said, in a muffled voice.

"Well, what is it, then? Hasn't any man touched your hands before?"

There was no answer to any of this, really. I did the only thing possible. Tugged away from his clasp, and ran, only I ran the wrong way. Up a slope that seemed to be the path we had been about to take. But it wasn't. I realized that. I heard him pounding up behind me, shouting, "Come back, Emma! Not that way!"

I couldn't stop. I didn't want to face him, and anyway, I was near the top. There was a break in the trees. I made for it. Heywood Stanton caught me round the waist just as I pulled up sharply, looking over into . . . nothing. Nothing but a sheer drop, down to the beach.

I did turn round then, gasping and shuddering at the thought of what it might have been, if I hadn't been able to stop my mad rush, if he hadn't been close enough behind me to hang on to me. I flung myself against him, clinging, terrified for a moment. "Oh, what a horrible place!" was all I could think of to say.

"It's my island," he said, between his teeth. "I suppose I'm horrible, too. Is that it?"

I don't know whether my face betrayed my thoughts or not. For one moment he held me fast to him. My hands were on his fore-arms, clinging. I was safe now, but I had forgotten to lose my hold. He was looking bitterly down into my face, and then his expression changed. Surprise, and then wariness crept into his eyes. I didn't understand it at all. I was too busy trying to analyse my own chaotic feelings.

He said, "We'd better forget this day, I think. And I also think I'd better do my own notes in future, and leave you to look after the children. I think we're overworking you," and gently but firmly he put me away from him, well away from him.

4

NOW I was really worried. I couldn't see what had gone wrong. I spent the rest of that day with the children in the dinghy. They were really good with that boat. Even young Timmy could be trusted to stay at the tiller, and both he and Jenneth were quick with their reflex action when Sheldon gave sudden sharp orders.

But my mind wasn't on the joys of tacking round the island. I kept thinking about Heywood Stanton.

Sheldon said, "You'd like to be put ashore, wouldn't you?" Such a shrewd comment from him told me that my puzzled thoughts showed.

"You haven't said if you enjoyed the trip round the island with Mr Stanton," Jenneth said primly. She wasn't angry with Heywood today because he had agreed to have the boat repaired.

"It was all right, but it's terribly artificial," I said, frowning. "I didn't like the waterfall

126

very much, for a start. I think Mr Ketwill shouldn't have tried to beautify the island."

They were all silent, and it occurred to me that they didn't know Colin Ketwill had been the former owner of the place nor that he had been responsible for the building of the waterfall.

Sometimes the children drew away from me, and exchanged secret looks with each other. It was like it all the next day, but I forgot, the day afterwards. It was such an eventful day.

It began with the meeting with the Macey boy. We were walking down to the South shore when he appeared. It was the first time I had seen him and I must say I at once shared the children's dislike of him. He was a weedy little brute with an overbearing swagger, an I-know-something-you-don't attitude that was particularly aggravating.

I muttered, "Take no notice," and tried to walk the young Holbrooks right past, but the main street through the island wasn't all that wide and the Macey boy blocked the path.

"If you don't let Miss Read go past, I'll knock your block off," Sheldon said quietly, in his best boarding-school voice.

"That'll do, Sheldon," I said quickly. "I don't think George will be such an idiot as to go on like a three-year-old."

It was meant to shame George Macey but it didn't. He merely grinned at me and offered the information. "I saw you in the woods with the Guvnor." And the way he leered at me, I was in no doubt as to the fact that he had witnessed that near embrace when I had run up the slope, Heywood haring after me. My face reddened fierily.

Sheldon glanced at me. He didn't know what that meant but it just added the spark to his always smouldering anger against the Macey boy. He hit out and floored George Macey.

It was so quickly done, I think it surprised Sheldon as much as the rest of us. Jen and Timmy danced around, triumphant, but the grown-ups came out, so I thought it best that we should go. I quickly explained to Oliver Cripley what had happened, and he grinned, but George Macey's father's face was more than angry. It was vengeful. It astonished me.

"That does it!" the man said. "I always

told him how it'd be, and it will be, see if it isn't."

"Now you take it easy," Cripley warned. I left them promising each other dire acts of revenge that struck me as being very childish.

Sheldon, however, was worried. "I shouldn't have done that," he muttered.

"Oh, go on," I said, slapping him on the shoulder, "It was a marvellous wallop — so neat, it took my breath away."

Sheldon still wasn't happy. "You don't understand, Emma," he said, as he trudged by my side. Sand got in his shoes, but for once he didn't make a fuss about it or put over a big-brother act because Timmy kept stopping to shake his shoes.

"Then *make* me understand, Sheldon," I fumed.

"I told you. We don't properly understand ourselves. It's to do with the grown-ups."

"We think — " Timmy began, but Jenneth shut him up. "I'll tell it," she said. "We think that that Macey boy's father *knows* something, and he's threatening Mr Stanton, just like on the telly."

"Oh, rot," I said. "You kids watch too much telly."

"What did he mean, Emma, about seeing you in the woods with Mr Stanton?"

"He was just being nasty. Mr Stanton rescued me. I almost fell off the cliff at the top of that hill. It's a horrid spot."

"Oh." Sheldon made the comment just like an adult would, as if he saw the rescue in his mind's eye and could see me in Heywood's arms. I blushed a fiery red.

"Well, it's got nothing to do with that horrid little beast," I said sharply. "Even if he did see us, which I don't believe."

"He climbs trees to snoop," Jen said, wrinkling up her nose.

"Tell you what, if I see him again, I'll . . . I'll knock him out again," Sheldon said heatedly, and he wasn't being boastful.

I thought about it. This secret they kept talking about, if Macey did know about it, and was insisting on living on the island with his boy, perhaps being paid for a job he wasn't really doing, that would amount to blackmail wouldn't it? But then that argued that Heywood Stanton had done something criminal, and such a thought I promptly dismissed. Bad tempered he might be, to say nothing of ill-mannered when he felt like it, bossy, overbearing, cynical, oh, there was no end of things I could tell myself he was: but not law-breaking. Never that.

We went down to where the dinghy was moored. Every time we did this I caught my breath, afraid that that Macey boy had done something else to it. And he had. "He's done it again!" Sheldon roared. "Look at it!" And this time even I could see the extent of the damage. There was a hole right through and the jagged woodwork sagged.

"But a boy couldn't do that, could he?" I asked, holding on to Sheldon to prevent him from doing anything rash.

"The tiller's gone, too," Sheldon said, unable to believe It. "Look at it — smashed to pieces! I don't believe it — I just don't believe it."

I couldn't hold him. He ran. The others wanted to go too, but I held them back and looked worriedly at the place where I had last seen Sheldon.

"Don't go too," I said quickly. "Stay with me. The grown-ups might reason with Sheldon, but if you *all* go — "

We walked on. Timmy was sobbing, and held on to me. After all, he was only six, but he knew this was serious enough to be frightened about it. I comforted him as best I could. "Let the big boys fight it out, Timmy," I said, but Jenneth said scornfully, "That Macey boy won't fight. He'll fetch his father, and if no one's about, he might do our Sheldon an injury. He nearly hit him with a long piece of wood once, only we came and shouted at him, didn't we, Tim?"

I hesitated. Perhaps I shouldn't have stopped them from going back. Perhaps I should have gone, too. I said, "Let's go back, then."

But there was no sign of either of the Maceys or Sheldon. I asked Oliver but he just said, "Don't interfere."

We were going over to King's Dassett. I couldn't wait for Sheldon any longer. The two young ones went with me, and as usual, examined everything in the shop before they decided what they would buy with the small coins I gave them, while I telephoned Nolan Pearce.

To my surprise and delight he was out of hospital. He said, "Where can you meet me?" but of course, with the children, I couldn't go much farther than the village.

He said, "All right, I'll come to King's Dassett. No, I'm not driving yet. It will be in a friend's car."

The friend turned out to be a girl, two or three years older than I was, and she worked in the Appointments Office of St John's Hospital. We found a lot to talk about while she drove us around, and then we stopped at an inn for soft drinks in the rose garden, Nolan told her to take the kids for a walk while he talked to me.

"She's a good sort," he said. I wondered if it was his girl-friend. He must have read my thoughts. "She's engaged to the houseman on the medical firm," he grinned.

He was as nice as I had first thought him, on the train. We had so much to talk about, and so little time. "Mr Stanton won't let you come over to the island," I warned, "and I have to have the children with me all the time. It's part of my holiday job."

"Can't they be left with someone while we go to the pictures or something?" he complained. So we thought about it and I said I'd ask.

"You've changed. The sun and air have changed you," he said.

"Do you like the change, or hate it?" I laughed.

"Oh, I like it. A tan suits you," he said. "When this wretched leg is completely better, why don't we go swimming? Would you like that?"

We wildly fixed dates to meet, which was silly. How did I know that I would be able to get away? But it was such fun, and so nice, to find a young man I could talk to, without having my head bitten off.

He said, "About Stanton, if you don't like it there, you must leave, Emma. I can arrange for you to go somewhere until you're ready to start at St John's, you know. I've got friends who could help you."

I shook my head. "Thanks, but I'd like to stick it out."

"Then you don't really dislike Stanton?"

"I didn't say that," I protested. "Well, let's put it this way. The job is a challenge. I know there's a secret he's fretting over. It isn't my business, really, but at the same time I don't have to run away because of it, do I?"

"No, you don't," he said, looking keenly at me. "Have you any idea what the secret is?"

"It's enough to make him keep strangers off the island, though he gets so frustrated with the way the local people run the house that he tries to get maids to come from Chighampton. He seems to want to be fair and reasonable, but then the secret nags at him and he gets really bad-tempered."

"If it will help, I can tell you what it is," Nolan Pearce said slowly. "What I mean is, it's not so awful that you need be afraid of it. But it's an awful thing for a man to live with."

"You mean . . . the Thing on the roof?" I said, unconsciously saying it the way the children said it.

Nolan looked startled. "*Is* there a Thing on the roof? Or have the children been getting at you again?" He laughed. "No, nothing so grim or dramatic, but really rather terrible in a way. I don't know if you know what Stanton was before he began writing."

"No, I don't," I said. "What has that got to do with it?"

"It has, a lot," Nolan said slowly. "It was before my time, of course, but people still talk about him. He was a surgeon."

I let out a long slow breath. "I thought

so. At least," I amended, "I saw him in my mind's eye in a long white coat when I tried to picture him at work before he came to the island." And then my hand flew to my mouth in dismay. "Oh!" I gasped.

"What's the matter, Emma?"

"Oh, what I said to him when I was in a temper once. He tried to dissuade me from being a nurse, and he told me a lot about the life there, and I asked him what *he* knew about it! Oh, what shall I do."

Nolan laughed comically. "Oh, dear. Poor chap! He was the youngest surgeon, they tell me, and on the way to a brilliant future, but there was a tragic mistake made. He couldn't take it. He just packed it in. It was his own cousin, they say."

"His cousin! The children said he used to come to their home to see their father, while they were away at school, and they mentioned that the cousin came as well, with his mother, Mrs Boyd."

"I don't know about that," Nolan said. "I heard that for some reason he couldn't operate on the cousin at once, and then it didn't turn out right. I also heard that if he hadn't been so sensitive about it, and told himself he ought to get out of the world of hospital, he could have put it right. I've heard of a lot of people saying they thought if he'd operated on the cousin again, it would be all right. New techniques now, and one thing and another. But of course, I suppose he's forgotten all he ever knew."

"And just for that," I marvelled, "he threw up a good career and came to the island to vegetate?"

"Is that what he's doing, Emma?" Nolan asked quietly.

"Well, no, not really. He's got a real feeling for history, Roman times, you know. But is that what a one-time surgeon wants? To sit in a study and write about people who have been dead for ten thousand years?"

"I wouldn't want that," he said at once. "But then, who am I? I want a private practice and a wife who can help me, and children of my own, and a practice filled with friends. In a country town like Chighampton," and he looked at me. "What will you want, Emma, after you've qualified?"

What would I want? I couldn't think any more. Not long ago I would have said unhesitatingly that I dreamed of having a ward of my own, but now all I could see in my mind's eye was the unhappy face of a surgeon who had operated on a relative and blamed himself for ever that it had gone wrong.

I was saved from answering by the return of the children. "Barbara's found some kittens in a new litter and the woman says we can have one each. Can we take them back with us now, Emma?" Jen screamed.

"Good gracious, no. I don't think it will be allowed anyway, but you can't have kittens at once from a new litter," I protested, and shook my head at Barbara over Jenneth's head.

"Wouldn't the Great Man allow it?" Nolan murmured.

"I seem to think we have our fair share of animals out there already," I murmured, thinking of the cat that had whacked me that first day.

It had been a lovely afternoon after all. Nolan arranged for at least three other meetings, before we went back to King's Dassett, and when I took Jen and Timmy back over the causeway, they were full of their new friend Barbara and what she had told them about her home and young brothers and sisters.

"You didn't tell her anything about Mr Stanton, did you?" I asked them.

They thought that was a very silly question. "Of course not!" they said.

I let them chatter while I thought about his tragic past, and I didn't know how I was going to face him again, now that I knew.

"We have to find your brother. Let's hope he's forgotten about the Macey boy," I said, wondering what Sheldon had been doing with himself. But we couldn't find him.

We asked Oliver Cripley to let them know at the house that we were back, and then we went in search of Sheldon. No sense in only two of them presenting ourselves at Moon House for tea.

The sea was running in. We were walking along the shore when Timmy suddenly said, "I can hear our Sheldon shouting!"

I couldn't. I could only hear the buffeting of the wind against my ears, but presently Jenneth said she could hear Sheldon, too, and both the children began to run.

I followed them, wondering what had happened now.

Sheldon was out on the rocks beyond the Point. "What's he doing out there?" Jenneth exclaimed. "He's not in his swim things. He's fully dressed. He's trying to rescue someone, I think."

"No, he's trying to push someone in," Timmy said with interest.

"What a lot of rot," I said, my heart beginning to pound as I remembered what a lot of bitterness there had been between Sheldon and the Macey boy. Not just a schoolboy hate, but real bitterness.

And there they were, Sheldon in up to his armpits, holding up the Macey boy. I had clambered over the rocks to get this view of them. I had told the children to stay on shore, but they swam so easily, it was second nature for them to come out and be in the thing. I said to Sheldon, "Can't you get him ashore?" It was so odd, the way he was holding him up.

Sheldon said in a peculiar voice, "I can't. I think he's broken something. I didn't want to hurt him any more." And as he spoke, I could see that there was blood on the boy.

"What happened," I gasped, as I edged down to where they were. It was deepish water between the rocks, but the sea was so calm considering it was running in. Given twenty minutes, it would be a boiling inferno here, and both the boys would be dashed on to the rocks.

"I think he must have fallen from up there," Sheldon said, "robbing a nest or something."

He was getting exhausted. He was thoroughly relieved when I took the weight and between us, we got him up to the ledge of rock, to where the other two had prudently climbed.

What I had learned in my sketchy times at the hospital, had stuck. I had seen something like this before, and without thinking, I said, "Go and fetch Mr Stanton at once, one of you. Say it's urgent."

"But what can *he* do?" Sheldon asked blankly. "Shouldn't we race over the causeway and telephone for a doctor."

I realized what I had said, but I stuck to it. "It's Mr Stanton I want, and I *don't* want Macey senior, so be sure he doesn't get wind of this yet."

The children nodded, and they all went.

"Tell him to bring the First Aid Box," I shouted after them and Jen raised a hand in acknowledgement.

That was as nasty a time as any I ever had. After the children had gone, the sea pepped up its rising. The wind grew brisker, and I rather wished I had kept Sheldon with me to help me move young Macey. Skinny he might be, but at the moment he was a dead weight, and I wasn't sure just how much of him had got injured in that fall. He was losing blood, too. All I could do was to rip off a clean white blouse I was wearing, and use it to staunch the area which was bleeding. The blouse was the only garment that hadn't got stained with the green slime on the rocks. I couldn't get off my clean white petticoat without letting the Macey boy slide off the rocks into the sea. So I waited.

Presently I saw Heywood Stanton coming down the edge of the sand, at the double, the children streaking after him, and behind them Oliver Cripley carrying an old door over his shoulder, no doubt to use as a stretcher. Behind him was Macey, the boy's father, and one or two others. My heart sank when I saw them.

But the minute Heywood Stanton arrived, everything seemed miraculously all right. He took one look at me, and peeled off his jacket. "Put this round you," he said curtly, "before the others come," and he took the boy from me. I did as I was told.

He examined the boy, beyond the reach of the sea, and pronounced no bones broken. Sheldon visibly brightened, but was puzzled. Macey senior kept on in a belligerent voice about who had done this to his boy, but I lost my temper. "If your boy would keep his hands off things that don't belong to him, like birds' nests and other people's dinghies, he wouldn't have got into this mess!"

Macey senior calmed down after that. So he knew about the dinghy! Heywood Stanton curtly told me to go back to the house and take a hot bath, and see to the children, too. But they, of course, had almost dried off, with their run to the house and back. The last I saw of Heywood Stanton was a business-like bit of cleaning up and bandaging.

The children walked soberly by my side. "How does he know what to do?" Jenneth couldn't resist asking, at last.

"Well," I said, improvising wildly, "you must have noticed that Mr Stanton is a very educated man, and probably knows about how to do a lot of other things one would never suspect. Anyway, he's only been bandaging and a lot of people can do that."

But Heywood Stanton had done more than that, and we all knew it, though we didn't know until later, just what. Oliver Cripley was telling Sheldon delightedly, when I came down from taking a bath, that the lad's shoulder had been put out, and Heywood Stanton had jerked it back again. "Cor, it was as nice a bit of work as ever I see, and the miserable little varmint didn't know a thing about it, him still being flat out."

The Macey boy had survived, but for the young Holbrooks there was the inquest to follow. Macey Senior would see to that. And for me there was even more hot water. Heywood Stanton sent for me later that evening.

"What happened?" he demanded.

"Sheldon told me," I began, but he cut across me. "No, I don't want to know what that boy told you. I want to know from you what happened. I have the boy's father on my back."

"Well, I don't know what happened, Mr Stanton. I wasn't here," I said, losing my temper again. If only I could have remembered in time to take my poor mother's advice. I always had, until I came to Moon Island and met Heywood Stanton!

"So, now we're coming to the crux of the matter," he said, in a low voice. "You've been let off working for me, so that you could keep the children with you all the time, and the very first day, you go off and leave them."

"Oh, no, I didn't. I had Jenneth and Timmy with me, but Sheldon had gone off to find the Macey boy. Well, Sheldon isn't a child, and this isn't the first time his boat has got damaged. I don't blame him for seeing red."

That, too, was the wrong thing to say. He tightened his lips and turned his back on me.

I couldn't keep silent. "Mr Stanton, I don't know why the Maceys are on the island. They don't seem to do anything useful and they keep taunting the children

— father and son. He's a horrible boy. If Sheldon hadn't stood up to him the other day then I would have done! Goodness, he stood square in my path! Sheldon knocked him out with a beautiful upper-cut."

I thought, I really thought, that Heywood Stanton would have been pleased. But he wasn't. "You will be good enough not to encourage my wards in such a lapse of behaviour," he said cuttingly. "And I am still waiting to hear what happened today. Where did you go? Who were you with?"

"I don't think I need tell you what I do in my spare time, Mr Stanton," I flashed. "I took the younger children with me, and I didn't have to. I would have taken Sheldon too, only I couldn't find him and I wanted to get over the causeway and back before high tide."

"What did you want to do in such a tearing hurry that wouldn't let you wait to find Sheldon? None of this would have happened if — "

"No, you're right!" I burst out. "If I had found Sheldon and taken him with me, the Macey boy would have been dead! Don't you see? He was climbing, interfering with the birds' nests on the cliff-face. Sheldon held him up and he was almost at his last gasp when I found him!"

The justice of this struck him. He didn't like being put in the wrong, though, and I knew he would hit back, and win. He always did. But I wasn't prepared for the body blow he dealt me. "Well, Miss Read," he said coldly, "perhaps you will be good enough to enlighten me on another point before I release you. When you wanted a doctor, why did you send for *me*?"

5

I WAS absolutely dismayed by that question. How my unruly tongue got me into difficulties with this man? I was conscious of his close-drawn dark brows, and his angry eyes, but mostly I noticed the little nerve that twitched in his cheek, and for the first time, perhaps, I noticed that when his mouth wasn't pulled into a thin hard line, it was a very sensitive mouth indeed. At this moment, beneath his anger and frustration, here was a very unhappy young man. And I, it struck me, was making the situation worse. It didn't matter that I didn't mean to; I just did, without even trying, and I wasn't surprised when he later told me rather bitterly that all this worsening of the situation had happened since I had come here.

I couldn't see any way out of it but to tell him the truth in answer to that shattering question of his. I could, of course, have said that I had sent for him as master of the house, to tell me what to do, but he knew and I knew that he knew, that that wouldn't answer. "Someone told me that you had once been a surgeon," I said, and considering my heart was in my mouth, my voice sounded singularly level and cool.

"Who?" he flashed at me.

"A doctor friend, at my old hospital," I said.

"Ah, yes, now we come to the crux of the matter. The person, I suppose, that you have such a pressing need to dash over the causeway to telephone. His name?"

I told him. There was no sense in refusing to, but of course, he had never heard of Nolan Pearce. Nolan was a young doctor, years behind a surgeon of the apparent standing of Heywood Stanton.

"So . . . what did he tell you?" he breathed.

I shrugged. "Not very much. He had found your name familiar and then remembered people talk about you, as having been one of the top surgeons, who had given up surgery when an operation went wrong." He whitened at that, so I said, "Did your cousin ever get right again? Nolan said people always insisted that if only you'd operated on your cousin again, it would have been all right, the latest techniques being what they are."

"My cousin!" he ejaculated. "Is that all he told you? Only about my cousin?" and he looked surprised.

"That's all. For me, it was enough. If you want to know, I could have died of shame on the spot when I remembered how rudely I spoke to you the day you told me about the tragic side of hospital life and I asked you what you thought you knew about it. I don't know how I could have. Is it any use apologizing now, Mr Stanton?"

He stared at me, and then an unwilling smile twitched at the corner of his mouth. "Well, you have, haven't you? You've eaten humble pie. So I suppose I must accept it with good grace. Don't hate me too much for making you do it, though, will you?"

Sometimes, as on this particular occasion, I found myself thinking that underneath, he must be a very human person. But as always, he turned again, and made me angry, before I had had time to savour the thought of how nice he could be. "But this won't alter the position," he said sternly. "Because of you, people are talking about me again. The old business will flare up because people have nothing else to do but gossip. And all my efforts to get away from it all, will have been for nothing! What do you think I feel about that?"

"Perhaps you shouldn't have striven to get away from it all," I retorted. "Sometimes getting away from it all is just another way of running away."

Really, I don't know how I dared. But at the time, I just wanted to help him. It was in no sense cheek, whatever he might have thought.

"I am grateful to you for your opinion," he said acidly. "Nonetheless, I would be glad if you would confine your holiday to the island, if you can't resist talking to strangers about me and my business."

"But I have your business at heart," I protested. "Forgive me, but did your cousin die?"

His mouth twisted, as if in pain. "No, my cousin did not die," he said heavily, almost as if he were sorry; "and to prevent you asking, in your zeal to help me, whether I did perform that second operation, the answer is that I did not." And I was so abashed at his tone and the enormity of the thing I had just asked him, that I just stayed dumb for once. Perhaps it was because he expected me to say something he wouldn't like, and was put out because I didn't, that he said, "I'll tell you about it, I think. Perhaps it will cure you of being inquisitive," and he looked so angry that I backed away from him.

Just as he was about to divulge what had happened, however, there was a diffident tap on the door and his mother opened it. "Oh, Heywood dear, I'm sorry, I didn't know you were working," she said.

It was so ludicrous. Anyone with half an eye could see that he was giving me the telling-off of all time. But his mother didn't allow it to show that she noticed that, if she did, that is. He waited patiently and she said, "I rather think you ought to come and settle Macey. Such a tiresome man. He has been objectionable to Mary Abbott and her father, and I don't want Mary to leave me."

With a muttered remark that I didn't catch, Heywood Stanton dismissed me and marched out after his mother. So I didn't hear, that day, what had happened to his cousin.

That information came in the oddest way. The following day a gale force wind tore over the island. The weather had broken in the night and in some measure the lashing rain and the wind compensated the children for the loss of their boat. For some reason best known to himself, Heywood Stanton had smoothed over Macey Senior and not charged him for the damage his son had done to Sheldon's little dinghy. Now I would have thought that with a temper like his, Heywood Stanton would have shaken Macey like a dog shakes a rat, and really chastised him over it. But no, all this being nice to the Maceys really bothered me.

"But why, why?" I asked Mrs Boyd. "It's a dreadful thing that horrible boy keeps doing, and here is our Sheldon saving his life, and Mr Stanton doing first aid on the boy, and no one giving a word of thanks. Only making more trouble, and Mr Stanton is appeasing them. Why?"

Mrs Boyd said, "It's not easy, my dear, to live on an island with someone objectionable like Macey and his boy. You've only seen Moon Island in good weather. Now it's changed and the causeway will be practically under water, you will see what I mean."

"Yes, but why keep Macey and his boy here? They're not natives of the island. They're strangers, and the people who always live here don't really like them."

"Don't they, dear?" She smiled faintly at me. "You sound so indignant on our behalf, it seems that you have well and truly dug yourself into the family. I'm so glad." She sighed. "But there, you will be off at the end of the summer holidays, and the days keep hurrying by and that time will soon be here."

"You sound, if I may say so, as if you don't want me to go," I ventured.

She nodded. "You're right, Emma," she sighed. "I don't want you to go. You're such a comfortable person to have around, and I can't think how you manage to create that impression, for my son tells me you have a sharp temper, but even so, he treats you differently to other people who have come here. You've made an impression on him, too."

"Oh, I know," I said, with a chuckle. "I've made him so livid that he can't bear me in his study with him sometimes. He says so."

"Yes, well," she said, biting her lip, "he has a lot of anxiety. A lot to put up with in many ways. But I'm sure you have a steadying influence." She looked at me. "It really is strange. It isn't as if you were, forgive me, at all intimidating or spectacular in your appearance. Such a quiet young woman . . . "

" . . . I know what I look like, Mrs Boyd," I said, with an amused smile. I could feel it lifting my face. It really was a joke to hear her say such a thing. "I've been told at school and at my hospital that I looked the clean-scrubbed type who appeals to all generations. I don't mind, you know. When you only want to be a nurse, you don't have to worry about nice clothes or make-up or glamour. You just want to . . . nurse," I said, on a low note, for it had suddenly struck me that I should feel different when I went to St John's, having met and seen daily a man who was a well-known surgeon and who had faded from the scene because of that strange thing that had happened.

"Don't mind when my son gets cross with you," Mrs Boyd suddenly urged. "He doesn't really mean it. He has to let fly at someone, and you fight back, which stimulates him. I've noticed that. I think you are good for him."

"He doesn't think so, Mrs Boyd. He said so. He has forbidden me to meet old friends on the mainland. Because of the person I telephone."

Her thoughts had wandered. She was staring out of the window at the sea sending up fascinating sheets of spray against the wall. "Oh, never mind, dear. You can go to the mainland when the weather eases up. I shall want you to execute some little commissions for me, anyway — Don't mind what my son says. He has his anxieties."

So had I. That day I had my work cut out, keeping the children amused. They were all over the place. Jenneth went out to run in the wind and rain and twice returned soaked to the skin. At last I put them in oilskins and boots, and walked them as far as I could, to get them tired. Of course, Sheldon never got tired, but sometimes he abandoned his endearingly grown-up big brother act and fooled about like the others.

We were walking along the South Beach, and I saw that the mainland was blotted out. I said idly, "What happens if someone is taken ill in weather like this? How do they get to the hospital?"

"We don't know how other people will manage," Sheldon said, rather unwillingly, I thought, "but we read about some people who were on an island and made a beacon and kept it covered so the rain wouldn't soak it. It fetches help if you set fire to it. We've made one on the highest point."

"But who would see it and come?" I thought, not really believing that the post-mistress would bother. It was in times of need that she suddenly remembered that she was an old woman whom nobody listened to.

Jenneth said smartly, "We've found out that the air-sea rescue 'copter from Chighampton can see our beacon, and they'd come right away. They like to, you know. It's practice for them. When they don't have accidents or distress calls, they throw a dummy into the sea and practise rescuing it."

Sheldon endorsed this. Timmy danced around, clamouring, "Let's fire the beacon now, and see if the chopper comes! Let's, let's!"

I wondered if anyone would need to do such a thing, now that I knew Heywood Stanton had been a surgeon. But of course, he wasn't practising any more, and perhaps if he weren't taken by surprise, he wouldn't even admit to it now. I had caught him on the wrong foot with the Macey boy and I didn't suppose he would forgive me.

The children raced ahead. I marched along thinking. How was it Mrs Boyd hadn't closely questioned me about what Heywood had been giving me a dressing down for? Did she know I had found out about his early career? I remembered the conversations I had heard between Mrs Boyd and her son, regarding his secret, and again I wondered who the occupant on the roof could be. If only I could believe the tales the children told. They had called her Aurelia, said she was a pretty girl who did peculiar things, and that her name meant 'the golden'. It sounded like a fairy tale that Jenneth had read. It occurred to me that they had never really seen the person on the roof and that they made up stories about that person to scare themselves. As to the Peeping Tom who was supposed to watch Aurelia, he was probably someone like that American tourist, who had been forbidden access to the island and was curious.

We had reached the last little cluster of cottages by then, and the children came running back to me. "Quick, Emma, you can practise your nursing — old Mrs Willis has fallen down."

"No, she's been beaten up," Timmy shouted, dancing around. "There's all blood everywhere. It's someone got on to the island and has beaten her up."

Apparently the other cottages were empty at this moment. Mrs Willis was lying in the open doorway of her little dwelling, and there was a lot of blood about, but when I investigated, I found that she was losing blood by the artery in her arm, and that she was still gripping the knife which she had apparently been using, when it had slipped. She must have gone to her door to shout for help, not knowing her neighbours were out.

I said, "Find me a stick, someone, I

must make a tourniquet. Go and find Mr Stanton, someone."

There were clean tea-cloths neatly folded in the dresser drawer. I began to tear them into strips. I worked just as I had been taught to, confidently expecting one of the children to come back with Heywood Stanton at the double. No matter how angry he would be, I wanted him here badly. I couldn't stop the bleeding, yet I was doing all the right things.

The gale had died down, but there was still sufficient wind to bring with it the smell of burning. I stopped my ministrations on old Mrs Willis and turned to see where the smoke was coming from. The sky was suddenly aglow, where it had been dull grey with racing clouds not so long back. Jenneth and Timmy came racing back.

"What have you done?" I whispered, suddenly realizing.

"We couldn't find that old Mr Stanton and you said it was life or death, so we fired the beacon for the chopper to take her to hospital."

I sat back on my heels, never relinquishing my hold on the twisted rags, and

I looked at them. Sheldon came running, his face white. "Who did it?" he shouted. "Which of you fired it?"

Jenneth and Timmy looked scared, because of the way Sheldon and I were looking at them, but they were too young to know the implications, and it was all my fault: I should have pointed those out to them when they told me about the beacon. I said slowly, "Mr Stanton doesn't want strangers here because of the secret. Every newspaper man in miles will come for a story when the chopper comes out."

The enormity of it all struck us dumb. We sat looking at each other. We hardly noticed Heywood Stanton, with Oliver Cripley behind him.

Heywood Stanton looked at Mrs Willis and dropped on to his knees beside her. "What have you done so far?" he asked me, and I told him. "How did it happen?" he asked, but I couldn't tell him that. I just said how we had found her. Again it was second hand: the children had found her. I had been some way behind. I would have to account to him for that later. I could see that from his face.

"I watched for the chopper and I can see it," Timmy shouted, racing back. We could hear it ourselves at that moment. It landed on the beach. I didn't see him do it but there were dark glasses hastily put on Heywood Stanton's nose before the pilot and the others dropped out and came running with their stretcher. Heywood Stanton found that she had broken her leg, too, and told the men, concisely, so that they glanced sharply at him but didn't comment. There was another man with them who didn't attempt to do anything to Mrs Willis but made notes in his notebook.

"If you're from the press," Heywood said, "I'll throw you into the sea, your notebook with you, if you don't destroy what you've written."

The man hastily backed away and went with the others back to the chopper. Oliver took the children back with him, leaving us to follow. He said he'd ask Mary to come over and clean up. I stood by Heywood's side. Both of us had blood on us now, and I felt cold. Cold with apprehension. The beacon was a red-gold glow against the purplish-grey of the heavy low clouds.

He looked at it. "Your idea, I suppose?" he said nastily.

I stood helplessly. How could I tell him that it was the children's idea and that they had set light to it? He said, "I might as well send every boat we possess to the shore and offer free passage to all the newshounds who will now want to come out here."

Of course, that sort of remark could never go unchallenged by an idiot like me. Oh, no, I had to snap smartly back, "What makes you think that your hermit-like existence is news value, Mr Stanton?"

I'll never forget the way his eyes rested coldly on mine, and held them. "Perhaps I'd better tell you why," he said.

The rain started again, too late to help us. The beacon fire was dying down anyway, but it plastered his hair to his head in tight little waves and made his thin face more skull like than ever. He didn't seem to notice the rain running down his face. To me, it looked as if it was tears, floods of tears, as he said, "The newspapers know me only as a surgeon who made a mistake, a costly mistake. As such, that wasn't hot news, except that the person who died under my knife was hot news at the time."

The rain now made running sounds, rushing down the little roofs of the cottages, and the sea smacking on the beach almost drowned the sound of his voice. "What they didn't know, and which they will now find out, is the rest of the story, and that will indeed make good reading."

I just stood and stared at him.

He said, "I hope your silence doesn't mean you aren't interested. I thought you were consumed with curiosity on that other occasion. I should have told you then, of course."

"Don't, if you'd rather not," I faltered.

"On the contrary, I think I shall rather enjoy telling you. Showing you, too. Come along. Let's see how you stand up to the sight of the awful truth."

He marched me back to the house, but after we had divested ourselves of our soaking coats, he said, "Don't let's change yet. The sight of our gory activities might bring interesting results."

"If you don't mind, I'd rather change," I said coldly. "I'm soaked to the skin. You may not mind such discomfort, but I do," and I broke away from him. Surprisingly, he caught my wrist and hung on to it.

"What I have to show you, and tell you, will take five minutes only. You can think about it afterwards, while you're changing," and as his was the superior strength, without an undignified scene, I had to go with him.

He took me up the back stairs. A spiral staircase, and counting, I realized, with thudding heart, that it led to the roof apartment.

I wondered where the children were, and if they knew about this. I was too upset to notice where the door had been which had led us to this staircase. When I was almost too dizzy to go further, and Heywood still hanging on to my wrist, we suddenly arrived, and he opened a door.

Shabby the rest of the house might be, but up here everything was gleaming bright, and new. Good carpets, nicely upholstered and new furniture — mirrors, and small objects lying about of real value. I could see that at a glance. A really sumptuous apartment.

I was very doubtful about our wet clothes, and said so. The sound of my voice brought out a woman who was dressed as a nurse but had the height and physique of a policewoman.

"Where is our little pet, Hilda?" Heywood asked her.

She looked doubtfully at me, and inclined her head.

We didn't have to go any farther into the apartment. A girl came out at the sound of his voice. I don't think I've ever seen a more beautiful creature. Of course, she was made up, but discreetly, and no make-up could account for that wonderful complexion or those beautiful pansy blue eyes, or that full, well-shaped mouth. She was tall and walked well, and wore a gorgeous house coat trimmed with fur. Her hair — golden, as the children had said — was apparently naturally wavy, and finished with tiny tight ringlets, softening the contours of her face.

I was standing a little behind Heywood Stanton so the girl didn't see me at first. Hilda blocked the rest of her view.

The girl's face crinkled up suddenly into laughter, childish laughter, and she pointed to Heywood's blood-soaked clothing and said, "Look! What a mess! All red!" she laughed just like a child, then she stopped laughing, because he wasn't joining her laughter. She pouted, and said, "Now I can't cuddle you, Heywood. Why don't you change into some nice things and come and cuddle me? Please?"

I looked at him. The little nerve was twitching again. I said, "Can I go now?"

I always do idiotic things, talk before thinking, things like that. He looked irritated at me, because she heard my voice and pushed Hilda out of the way. The golden girl's beauty could vanish in an instant, it seemed. Hatred, childish hatred, filled her face, as she glared at me.

"Who's that?" she shouted. "I don't like her! She went swimming with you, Heywood. You like her, don't you? I'll — I'll — " she threatened, and childlike, all she could think of was to throw something. It was a biggish vase. I ducked and it smashed into a thousand pieces against the closed door behind me. And that made her cry. Evidently she had liked that vase. I didn't wait for anything more to happen. I turned and ran.

Sickened, oddly sickened because she was so very beautiful, I kept on running, round and round, down the spiral staircase. I didn't stop to listen to anyone's footsteps behind me, yet Heywood Stanton couldn't have been far off. He caught me up when I hesitated at the foot of the staircase. I couldn't see where to go. There was no door that I could see. But there must have been one somewhere.

He pushed against a wall that looked like the others — covered in a wallpaper that was composed of square patterns. It was the pattern that hid the door — purposely, no doubt.

He led me out and showed me a staircase I knew, up into the main part of the house. "Go and get a bath and change, and come to the study. I don't intend to let you get the wrong impression about all this. It isn't what you think, you know."

"Oh, isn't it!" As usual I spoke first and then regretted it when I had time to think. "What sort of an idiot do you take me for? She's the Thing on the Roof, that Timmy talks about. The golden girl that a Peeping Tom on the shore looks at through field glasses."

His face was terrible. I couldn't have hurt him more if I had tried. He looked stricken, but he stuck to the orders he had given me. "Bath and change, at the double.

I'll wait for you in the study."

All the while I took a hot bath, I wondered if he had not known about the children finding out, if he hadn't even known about the Peeping Tom. He wouldn't let me go on shore now, surely? And yet how could he keep me a prisoner? After all, I was going to leave the island, to go to work in a hospital where he had once been known. He couldn't stop me going, and he ran a shocking risk of his secret getting everywhere. I wondered if he were sorry that he had ever met me.

I changed into a clean dress, briefly looked in on the children and found that Mrs Boyd had personally supervised their hot baths and supper. Even Sheldon had been dispatched to bed, with a tray and permission to read for an hour later than the others, which mollified him. I said, "I have to go to the study, Mrs Boyd. Mr Stanton wants me."

"Yes, I know, dear," she said quietly, so I supposed that Hilda had told her what had happened. I didn't wait for any more, but ran downstairs.

I don't pretend that I felt very brave, as I tapped on the study door. My heart was thudding, and my legs felt decidedly jellyish. Heywood Stanton was pacing up and down. I could hear him. He said curtly, "Come in!" and surely there was never a more unwelcoming invitation.

I thought, as I went in and shut the door behind me, that he must have aged ten years. His face seemed thinner, that sensitive mouth of his was in its straight hard line like when he was angry, and he didn't look at me.

"Well," he said, "you have seen my cousin, and you were sickened."

"Your cousin!" My obvious surprise caught him and he turned to look at me then.

"You didn't know?" he asked. "But you've been talking about my cousin!"

"I thought it was a man, the way people mentioned the relationship," I faltered. "I didn't think it was a girl, such a beautiful girl, too."

"You can say that about another female, without any bitterness!" he observed. "It's a pity, Emma, with such an unusual personality, that you are so inquisitive."

"That's a word that you use to apply to people who like other people and want to help them," I retorted.

He let that go. He suddenly looked very tired. "Oh, come and sit down, do, so that I may sit," he said wearily, so I took the chair that I used for taking notes, and waited.

He said, "If I had operated on her right away, it wouldn't have happened."

I looked puzzled. I know I was looking puzzled, because he caught my eye, and he said, "Well, you must know what led up to it all. Surely?"

I shook my head. "It's all bits and pieces. The children know there's a secret, because people stop gossiping when they are near. They think it's about their father, who died when he was ill. I have heard people say it was a tragedy that you don't let the children know about."

He sat staring at me morosely, waiting for me to say it all. I went on, "People are so sorry for you when they talk about you. It doesn't tie up with your own self-condemnation. I don't understand it. Mr Ketwill seemed to like you very much but to allow that a tragedy happened. Mary Abbott started to tell me and then stopped herself, before she got very far. It's always the same. But I thought it was about your cousin, who should have been operated on again."

Still he stared at me, waiting. I continued, "But you said that someone died under the knife, at your hands. Is that another mistake you made? I don't understand any of it."

"Are you sure that that is all people have told you?" He looked a little less weary, I thought, as if he were mildly but pleasantly surprised.

"Yes, I'm sure. I'd tell you — you know me. I blurt out everything. There's no stopping me."

Briefly the smile twitched his lips, because he found my own condemnation amusing, I suppose. But it fled before it was born. He said, "There was an accident, in Aurelia's car. She was driving. She was in a wilful mood. The children's father had wanted to get to the station but the only taxi was out. She said why didn't he let her drive him? The answer was obvious — he didn't think much of her driving. He never had. He was my best friend," he said, his voice breaking. "But he had no tact or patience with Aurelia. And

172

she knew it. She was nettled, I suppose, and drove really recklessly, and crashed into a lamp standard."

"Oh, no!" I exclaimed. I thought of that girl with her youth and beauty, but a child's mind. A child's wilfulness. Was that what the accident had left?

He was sitting rock-still. Anyone else would have ducked his head in his hands or shouted or paced up and down, but not Heywood Stanton. He had, for his own reasons, set himself to tell me the whole story. It was tearing him apart to do so, but he sat rock-still and concentrated on the telling.

"Holbrook and Aurelia were both desperately badly injured, about the head mainly. I was at St John's at the time. It had been a day of accidents. A very bad day. And most of the staff had at last gone off duty. It so happened, by a set of curious circumstances, that I was the only one there. I had to make the decision, a split decision, which one to do first, until someone else could be fetched."

His knuckles shone white. "Heaven help me, I started on Holbrook. I thought he was in the worst case. I had to make a decision but I made the wrong one. He died during the operation. And Aurelia is as she is today, because she wasn't operated on soon enough." He thumped the desk suddenly with his fist. "So now you know!"

He looked at me as he said it, and for a moment our glances were locked. I didn't know that horror was all over my face — horror at the thought of the cross he had carried since that time. But he was facing me. He could see my face, and he read the wrong thing into it. He said, "I knew you wouldn't understand."

6

AFTER the storm, the weather came in mild and sunny and good. The reporters came out, but Mrs Boyd saw them. I don't know what she told them but miraculously the local papers only carried the story of the dramatic rescue of the old woman by helicopter, and they played up the children's part in it, how they had had the forethought to light the beacon. They also got the story of Sheldon's rescue of George Macey — a brilliant stroke on the part of Heywood's mother. I saw her suddenly in a new light; amiable and easy-going on the surface, but a veritable tigress when it came to defending her beloved son. I was chastened.

But of me, Heywood saw nothing. He kept right out of my way. He hadn't even asked me not to tell anyone what he had told me. It was as if he didn't care.

I thought, over and over again, of that scene in the study, and I asked myself, again and again, what else I could have done. I had had the absurd desire of rushing round the desk to put my arms round him nd comfort him, but of course I did no such thing. At all times be was very much the boss, and he would have torn a strip off me for any such performance.

I did say, without much tact I now saw, "Well, you could have tried to operate on her later, couldn't you?" It was awful. I was trying to help, but it was the worst thing I could have said. I could see, feel in every part of me, the shocking strain he had been through, the grief at losing his friend through his cousin's wilfulness, and the botch he had made of trying to save at least one of them. I could see, too, what resistance he had put up to this truly terrible stroke of Fate, that he should have found himself in such a ghastly situation. It might have been possible, I supposed, that a junior surgeon might have helped, but it was not a job for any junior surgeon. I supposed, seeing in my mind's eye, that frightful day in Casualty, that most of the surgeons were flat out, drugged with much needed sleep. I wondered if such things would happen when I went there, and it seemed to me more and more that I had chosen the right thing for me. It didn't fill me with distaste, whatever he might think. I was just all the more eager to go. But his personal tragedy filled me with a private grief, because the time for sparring with him had gone, and now all I wanted to do was to try and help him. Reach out to him, somehow. But of course I couldn't. He wouldn't let me. I saw, too, that he would never have let anyone help him.

Moon Island was not only the right sort of place for him to have retreated to; it was also, in its queer way, symbolic of his life. A place of beauty, terrifying beauty, like that girl on the roof, but a place to be kept hidden from all other eyes.

My heart bled for him. I said to Mrs Boyd, "Your son has told me about Aurelia, and the children's father, and what happened."

She flinched, but nodded. He had probably already told her he had done so. I said, "Of course I won't breathe a word to anyone, and I do understand why the children weren't allowed to know."

Again she nodded.

"But you do know, don't you, Mrs Boyd, that they realize there is a secret, because it apparently was in the newspapers at the time, and people gossip on the mainland about it, and break off when the children appear."

"I thought as much," she said flatly.

"And I think they are planning to find some old newspapers. They are always trying to get to the library at Poltoncross," I ventured.

She stared at me. "Are they?" she asked blankly.

"I'm telling you, because they may come on the information and I wouldn't like you or Mr Stanton to think that I had told them," I said earnestly.

"No, I do see that. Thank you, Emma." She put a weary hand to her head. "So much has happened. I can't believe that we've staved off publicity so far. Well, we must think," she said. "The children must not go on the mainland. After all, there is plenty for them to do here. If I need anything, you must go alone for me. And of course, you must have a day off once a week. Yes, you must," she said, as if assuring herself that much as she would have liked to keep me a prisoner on the island, that wouldn't be possible.

I didn't realize then, that she had her own private worries. I never seem to catch on at the time, or perhaps it was because my own mind was filled with thoughts about Heywood Stanton. Anyway, things rather boiled up the following day. She had been writing one of those letters to the person called 'Darrell' and had left it lying around. Heywood found it and there was a frightful row.

I heard it outside the door — she had sent me upstairs for a letter to be answered and I had just come back — and he shouted distinctly, "Mother, I told you I won't have him here, and if you don't know that also means don't communicate with him at all, then I must say so here and now."

"But Heywood, dear, you can't prevent me from writing to him," she said gently. "Be reasonable."

"Well, I can and I am. If you write to him it will go a stage further and he will come here to the island and when that happens, what then?"

She didn't answer. I went away, wondering what her silence could mean. I had the uneasy feeling that she was not the sort of person to do as Heywood said. Whoever this Darrell was, Mrs Boyd would have him to the island if she wanted him.

I wondered who on earth he could be. I strove to remember what she had said in all those letters which I had written to Darrell. He had lived in Poltoncross. I wondered then if he was the reason the children had been so keen to get to Poltoncross, when all the time I had thought they wanted to get to the Public Library there, to look up old newspapers about their father's death, and the secret in Heywood Stanton's life.

Well, I knew the answer to all that, later that day. The house was very quiet. Oliver Cripley had taken the children fishing in his boat, with special permission from Mrs Boyd. I didn't know where Heywood was but I had a sick certainty that he was on that roof-top, with that beautiful girl. Her beauty filled me with distaste, and I didn't know why. This was no way for a future nurse to feel. I spent the day roaming about the place trying to examine my own feelings. It was the sight of Heywood coming in for his fishing rod, and going out again, that gave me the answer. My heart gave a savage jolt, and

I knew, with self-loathing, that I wasn't feeling hateful towards that girl, for her beauty, but because she had first claim on Heywood. I must be in that state known as being in love.

I sat in a window seat and thought about it. I had had lots of boy-friends, but on a sports basis. Boys who liked to play a hard game of tennis with me, and sought me out for that purpose; boys who liked to go ice skating with me, and lately Dr Pearce who liked to talk to me about the hospital and that future practice of his. I had liked Nolan Pearce very much and it was a healthy liking. I had looked forward to seeing him again. What I had felt for him was nothing like this devouring emotion I had for Heywood Stanton. This was such an uncontrollable, overwhelming, untamable emotion. I could no more stop it or regulate it than I could stop or regulate the sea. It was as terrible as the sea, because it was unwanted, and bigger than myself. I don't even know when it started. I hadn't even liked him at first. But I had become intrigued, and I had liked sparring verbally with him. I felt more flashes of temper against him than against anyone else in my life that I could remember. I had come to admire him for his ruthlessness, and I had felt something special towards him because we had shared the same passion for history, particularly of Roman times.

All that seemed to have built up into this, topping it through the sudden knowledge that he had been a surgeon. And now I was jealous of that poor creature up there in the roof! It didn't bear thinking about. Nor did it bear thinking about that my new compassion for him, following on his telling me his secret, had brought with it a new sensation; I longed to physically comfort him, and I was just filled with a dull despairing ache because I knew that such a thing would not be possible. He was my employer, and anyway, I would soon be going away, out of his life.

A man's footsteps went quietly upstairs. I raised my head, listening. Instinctively I knew it wasn't Heywood. His footsteps made my heart bump and bounce in the most erratic way, just as the touch of his hands on mine made my pulses leap. No, this was a stranger, and a stranger could only mean that a newspaper reporter had got in.

Without stopping to think, I quietly went up the stairs after him, but I had lost him. I searched everywhere, until I found a door was ajar. I went through and found it was another way leading up to that flat in the roof. All was quiet up there, until I reached the top, and then there was such a commotion, I felt sick with anxiety. It had the quality about it of that time when Aurelia had thrown the vase at me.

Apparently she was doing it again. There was a series of crashes, and then running footsteps, and Hilda's strong voice, trying to soothe Aurelia and at the same time protesting to someone else that he had no business to come there the minute her back was turned.

The door flew open and a man reeled out, holding his head. There was a trickle of blood running down the side of it, which he was mopping with a white silk handkerchief. On his lips played a rueful smile.

"Not to worry! She'll be glad to see me next time," he said to Hilda. "She usually is. She gets bored, you know!"

Hilda growled something in reply and

slammed the door, bolting it. Then the man looked up and saw me.

I got quite a shock. He was so like Mrs Boyd in looks — that roundish bland face, those quiet light brown eyes, the lot — it was quite clear he was related to her.

"Hello," he said. "Who the devil are you and what are you doing here?"

"You're Darrell," I murmured.

"That's right. Darrell Boyd, and I have a right to be here. But have you? That is the question."

He was a youngish man, not more than twenty-five, but his eyes were bold at times. I didn't like him much. "Oh, yes, Mr Boyd, I have. I am the person who types those letters Mrs Boyd sends to you at Poltoncross."

He looked surprised, then smiled. "Well, well, well, so this is little Emma," he said, laughing. "Oh, I've heard a lot about you. Now, why don't we go somewhere quiet and have a nice little chat. You might be the answer to a very pressing problem I happen to have."

I think I knew very well what his problem would be. He looked the type to be always without money, always on the cadge. Easy come, easy go.

"I don't think we have to find any quiet corner, Mr Boyd," I said. "All I want to know is why you were up there upsetting Aurelia. You're not even supposed to be on the island, you know."

He leaned against the banisters, hands in pockets, and regarded me. "Well, now, we do take on airs, don't we? Hasn't my mother told you perfectly well that I may come here when I choose?"

"Your mother!" I ejaculated. Somehow I had never thought of him being her son. Two sons, each by a different marriage? Well, that could be, I supposed, trying to do hasty arithmetic.

He helped me. "I am just four years junior to dear Heywood, to save you wearing out that perky little head of yours. Dear Heywood loathes me thoroughly, because you see, I know a thing or two about him, and I wouldn't hesitate to trade in that knowledge, if he didn't play the game. Of course, he's darned mean — I never can screw much out of him these days. How much does he pay for your services, by the way? Yes, your wages, my girl, might just make up the difference."

I didn't think so. I believed that Mrs Boyd paid me what little I earned here, but I wasn't going to say so. I said angrily, "You have no right to discuss your half brother like this with me, a total stranger and an employee."

"Oh, but you asked me!" he retorted, looking vastly amused.

"No, I didn't!" I indignantly repudiated. "I asked you what you were doing in Aurelia's apartment, upsetting her!"

"Same thing, dear," he said coolly. "I can't get anything out of Heywood nowadays because all his cash goes into that apartment, so, in sheer common sense, I go there to collect!" and as he spoke, he took out of his pocket a small group in porcelain. I didn't know much about porcelain, but even to my untutored eye — as if his careful wrapping of it in his handkerchief wasn't enough to assure me! it was a treasure. "You're not going to sell that! That belongs to Aurelia!" I exploded. "Fancy taking things from someone like that!"

He looked thoughtfully at me, then put the thing, wrapped all carefully, back into his pocket. "Don't try to be naïve,

186

dear," he begged me. "You couldn't be that innocent. I don't take things from Aurelia. She gives them to me, willingly, in return for cuddling. But today it just happens I didn't want to stay. I'm in a hurry to catch the tide, and to be frank, I'm not much enamoured of kissing in that quarter. So she tried to do me a mischief on the way out," and he laughed, touching the deepish scratch which was now drying up. "I'm an expert in ducking, though," he said.

I thought about it, was disgusted, and no doubt showed it.

He didn't like that. "Oh, now don't you pretend to be a good little girl," he said, coming down to my level. "You wouldn't stay on this island if you weren't getting something out of it, *I'm* sure!" and he stood there, laughing softly at me. "Old Heywood has plenty of what it takes, if someone can stir him up, and I bet you stir him up all right."

I didn't stop to think. My hand came up sharply and the sound of the slap I gave him, sounded like a pistol shot. I heard footsteps. Mrs Boyd looked up the stairs. "What in the world — " she began, and then she took in the situation in a glance. I had turned and was hurrying down the stairs, and Darrell Boyd was still standing there with his hand to his stinging cheek. I glanced back as her eyes widened, and I saw, even from where I was standing, the imprint of my finger marks. That must have been the smack of all time, but then he angered me so deeply with what he had said about Heywood and me, that I didn't know I could be so angry. Mrs Boyd fell back and let me go by.

As I hurried on downstairs, I heard her say wearily, "I begged you not to come, Darrell. I begged you not to come!" and I heard his reply, lazy and a little amused still. "I know you wrote to me saying don't come, darling, but you omitted to put in the letter the amount I was coming for. So I . . . *had* to come!"

I was sorry for her. She loved both her sons so much, and it couldn't be nice to know how much they loathed each other and with such good reason. I wondered how much he would get for selling that piece of porcelain. A lot, I supposed, if it were a private sale to a friend.

I went out to walk in the wind. Now

I knew what the pressures were behind everything that happened. No wonder the children could feel them and called it 'a secret'. To them it must be upsetting, taking away their security. I was glad they were to go back to school at the end of the holidays.

It occurred to me that I ought to do the things they wanted me to, if they had to stay on the island: things like climbing to the top of the waterfall and visiting Black Valerian's cave, and learning to use their dinghy. As I passed by Oliver Cripley's cottage I noticed that he and another man were making strides, repairing it. More money out of poor Heywood's depleted pockets, I supposed. Why did he let that Macey boy get away with it, I wondered? And then I knew. Like Darrell Boyd, Macey Senior must have found out what had happened, and was threatening to expose Heywood. But would it be such an exposure, I wondered?

I pondered the point. Now that I knew the secret, would Heywood mind very much if it got out? Or did he trust me, and would therefore take the same precautions as before? Somehow I couldn't see him being afraid of what people would say about what he'd done. He just wanted to hide so that he shouldn't always be reminded of it. Well, that was all I could think of.

Meantime, I had to somehow get to a telephone booth to call up Nolan Pearce and cancel all those wildly improbable dates we had made. And I should, too, let poor Mr Ketwill know. He had arranged to meet me at tea in Chighampton the following day, for one of our chats. He really seemed to enjoy them.

The tide was receding. I could get across the causeway by paddling. I slung my shoes round my neck and ran, hoping the children wouldn't see me and try to come with me.

Nolan Pearce was bitterly disappointed. "Why can't you come, Emma?" he demanded. "It's only a holiday job! Well, for heaven's sake, if it's a case of looking after the kids, bring them along too. I don't mind. We can keep an eye on them between us."

"It isn't," I said, wishing I could tell him all about it. "I've been asked to stay on the island all the time, except for one day a week shopping for Mrs Boyd. It's because of the tourists who keep pestering us. And because of what the children might let out."

"Oh, that great secret! I can't imagine that Stanton would really care about people knowing. All he'd be afraid of was that the brutes might brave the causeway and invade his paradise."

"Well, whatever it is," I temporized, "it's their home, and they are my employers and I have agreed. Perhaps I could see you more often when I leave here and start at St John's. I shall need a friend."

"Must I wait so long, Emma?" was Nolan's wistful reply.

I hated leaving it at that, but there was nothing else that I could do. I next telephoned Colin Ketwill's hotel.

I don't know, I can't think why I should have been so shocked. I knew he had a bad heart condition, but when they told me that he had died in the night, I felt that someone had hit me. I couldn't believe it. I repeated my request and they had to tell me again.

"He wanted you told, miss, if anything happened to him, but you are not so easy to contact," they said reproachfully. "There is a letter on the way. It was the only way you could be contacted."

Yes, the local people must be pretty frustrated to think that nobody could reach a person on Moon Island to say that a friend had died. I choked on the words I had to say. The chauffeur came to the telephone to speak to me, but he, too, was too choked. He gave it up. He didn't know what was to happen to him and the ancient Rolls. Colin Ketwill had nobody belonging to him.

I stumbled back across the causeway. For once I wasn't struck by the beauty of the almost still sea, nor the silvery sheen on it. The island looked a hostile lump rising out of the mist, and I almost hated it.

I didn't even see Heywood standing at the end of the causeway watching me. He took me by the arms. "What's the matter, Emma?" he demanded.

"Matter? What do you mean?" I stammered.

"You're crying," he said tersely, and ran the back of his hand gently up my cheek. His hand came away wet.

"Oh. It's Mr Ketwill. He died last night. He was my friend," and then I was crying in earnest, and once I had started, I couldn't stop.

"Well, he had a heart condition, I think you said," Heywood murmured. "A fine nurse you're going to make!" He meant to rally me, but it scared me. Would I really be any good if I went to pieces like this when an old patient died, especially if I had let that person become a friend?

"Here, you can't stand bawling in full view of all the windows. Let's go and sit down somewhere," and he led me to a clump of rocks lying against the sea-wall. We sat down on the far side of them, so that we were at least sheltered from view of the house. He kept his arm round my shoulders, and he talked to me, on a sort of toneless note that was infinitely soothing. It almost put me to sleep.

"I know how you feel. Don't think I don't, Emma. I've seen death a good many times, and there's no way of not being affected by it, if you care. But if it's any use to you, I seem to remember hazily a saying by some bishop or other, about death merely being an horizon, and an horizon is just something that hides things from our sight. It might just help you. I don't know. As a boy, just losing his father, I found it comforting. You may not believe this, knowing me as a bad-tempered brute who uses you as a whipping boy for all the irritations other people serve me with, but I used to talk to my father every night, believing he was just beyond the horizon and listening to me. Not out loud, of course, but whispering, beneath the bed-clothes, so nobody else heard me. The things one does, when one is young and alone!"

I lay still against him, my crying finished. He was so comforting, I wondered how I could have thought all those angry thoughts about him. I said nothing, for fear of breaking the spell. It took such a little to let that steel shutter fall down over his face, and a stranger stand there in his shoes.

He talked to me about his boyhood, at school and in the holidays. He liked to go fishing. He made friends with the men taking out the boats and he liked being with them, when he should have been in bed. With Darrell Boyd, I wondered? He didn't mention him, or his step-father. And I hadn't the courage to ask.

"One learns a lot about life, on the sea

at night, Emma," he said quietly. "There's an old prayer, which goes something like this: 'Guard me, Lord, this night, for the sea is so wide and my boat is so small'. A fisherman's prayer. I know how he felt, when I used to watch the stars reflect themselves in the sea, and the land was only a thin smudge on the sky-line. Somehow one meets the truth, at times like that."

I wondered how he had met the truth of what he had done, by thinking of the stars on the sea. He had run away from everything, hadn't he, coming here? What if he had caused his best friend's death? No, not caused it — his cousin had caused it. The lovely Aurelia, which meant golden, as the children had told me. She had caused it, poor Heywood had merely done his best to save a life, and lost it. What did it feel like, to be in that position, I wondered, for the hundredth time?

Suddenly he looked down at me. "Oh, well, now I can stop my lecture, can't I, because you're all right now. Up you get! If you haven't anything to keep you busy, I can find you plenty."

I stumbled to my feet. That was Heywood — be nice to me for five minutes, and whip me around for fifty. I said tartly, "I haven't been without a pressing job to do since I came to Moon Island."

He grinned. "Ah, the tone of your voice tells me you are completely recovered. Right, well, you'd better just come back to the study with me and collect some notes I want done later. Take the portable up to your room and do them later."

"Portable! Portable, you call it? It weighs a ton," I said indignantly.

"No need to be rude about my dear old typewriter. I suppose I am strong enough to carry it up to your room for you," he said coldly.

I was going to let him, until I remembered that Boyd was still up on that floor somewhere. "Oh, no, don't come up with it. It doesn't matter — I'll find a time to do the notes in the study when you're not there," I said hastily, my cheeks flaming.

"Now what made you change your mind like that?" he asked suspiciously. We had been climbing the steps to the house. He stopped dead, his fun leaving him, his face going drawn and stony again. "Come on, Emma, out with it — why mustn't I be up on your floor?"

I bit my lip and tried hard on the instant to find an excuse to explain my reluctance all of a sudden to have the typewriter brought up by him. It was no use. I couldn't.

"Let's go up and see what's going on, to make you look so guilty," he said quietly. "I call to mind that the children weren't with you."

"You told me they weren't to leave the island!" I flashed at him.

"I know that. I don't believe I said you could leave the island in working hours, did I?"

"No, but your mother did!" I said unwisely. "Just before I went out."

"Now how did you come to see my mother?" he wanted to know. "I happen to know she had retired to her room with a splitting headache from which nothing will usually arouse her. Now just what is going on?"

It was no use. From that nice interlude on the shore when he had comforted me, things had suddenly and disastrously deteriorated, simply because of the typewriter.

Disaster on disaster followed. We were nearing my floor, with Heywood telling me coldly that he supposed the children were up to something and that I knew about it, when we suddenly heard a commotion. Hilda, and of all people, Heywood's mother. Their voices cut the air with a sharpness of deep anger. I couldn't believe it. Of Hilda, yes, perhaps, but of Mrs Boyd, no! But it was her shouting.

Heywood hurried forward, demanding to know what the trouble was. He looked up the stairs at the same time and saw the door leading to Aurelia's apartments standing wide open. "I seem to remember that I gave orders for that door to be shut and bolted at all times," he said.

I thought of stupid things, like the proximity of that door to the door of the sewing-room, which explained why the children weren't allowed to be up there with me. I felt a wretched cold lump in my middle and I dare not look at Mrs Boyd. The trouble seemed to be about her son Darrell.

"He came here?" Heywood thundered.

Mrs Boyd said angrily, "Yes, he did. He's also my son, and I wanted to talk to him. But it didn't mean that I condoned what he did."

Heywood looked at Hilda. "I made him give back the porcelain figurine that he persuaded Aurelia to give him. She was upset and didn't know what she was doing. He wanted to sell it!" she said indignantly.

"No, he didn't. She gave it to him as a present and I wasn't referring to that," Mrs Boyd said heatedly.

"Then what *were* you referring to, Mother?" Heywood asked quietly. So very quietly.

I said, "I'll go and find the children," and escaped. Such scenes sickened me. He called me to come back but I wouldn't listen. I ran and ran with my head down, first to Oliver Cripley's cottage, and then to the far shore where they had liked playing so much. But they weren't anywhere and nobody had seen them.

On the way back, Oliver Cripley said, "If I didn't know better, I'd have said — Oh, well, no, I'm speaking out of turn," and he reddened.

"I've got to find them, Mr Cripley," I said desperately, and it was then that I began to wonder where Aurelia was. Her door had been wide open. How was it she hadn't come out to see what all the fuss was about?

"Mr Cripley, have you seen Mr Darrell Boyd since he came to the island today?"

He looked relieved. "Oh, then, you know, miss. Well, then, perhaps it was all right, seeing as she was with him, I mean. If she'd been by herself, well, then — but there, she was with him and he was holding her pretty firmly by the arm and I was thinking to myself, about time that pretty creature got out and about a bit, so long as someone got hold of her pretty tight, if you see what I mean."

"Where did they go?" I asked tersely. "I'm sure she's not supposed to be out."

He looked alarmed. "Oh, isn't she?" His mouth hung stupidly open. "I did wonder if it was right — I mean, I just looked up and caught sight of a chap on the causeway only the next time I looked, it turns out to be Mr Stanton on the shore with you, miss," and he looked confused. No doubt he had been an interested spectator when I was crying and Heywood was comforting me. And then the full implication of his remark hit me.

"You mean — Mr Darrell went ashore,

alone? On the causeway?" I gasped, and he nodded. "When?" and when he thought, and hazarded a guess, that just must have been when Heywood was marching me up to my room to see why I didn't want the typewriter carried up.

"But where could she be?" I said, thinking. "And the children — would she — would she hurt them?"

Oliver Cripley looked unhappy. "I don't know, miss," he admitted.

"Well, I'll just have to search," I said, and I struck inshore. A voice shouted after me. It was Heywood, running. I shot down the steps again and made for the jungle in the middle of the island. I didn't want to be ordered back into the house by him in front of Oliver Cripley.

The comforting sound of hammer knocking nails, as he mended the children's dinghy, receded as I plunged further into the trees. Underfoot the ground was swampy. I didn't know where it led to. I just kept looking for a sight of that beautiful golden head. What would she do, after being imprisoned for so long, in the care of someone like Hilda? And what made me think I could persuade her to return, when

I knew nothing of her habits, her ways, beyond the fact that when she couldn't get what she wanted on the instant, she threw things, regardless of the possible damage to life and limb. Like a child, she followed her instincts, her wilful desires. Where would she go?

Of course, I wasn't prepared for it when I did find her. She had slipped on a green scarf over her hair, and she was wearing a green dress, and between them, those two garments had almost rendered her invisible until she turned and I saw her face.

I stood still in my tracks. For the first time I asked myself what I thought I could do, what I thought I could say to persuade her to return, considering I was the one she hated most. I followed her silently, wondering if she had realized I was there. She was looking pleased, as a child would on managing to escape from a locked room, a room for punishment. Perhaps she thought of her time in the roof apartment as a punishment! I couldn't imagine what she felt about the stalwart Hilda. I had never seen them converse together. Hilda always seemed to refer to Aurelia as an impersonal object, as an adult will about a child who cannot yet speak or understand. Aurelia might well have understood only too well, and had made her plans accordingly. Well, she had escaped, and I couldn't see or hear anything of Heywood who had been running after me.

Nor did I. Aurelia reached the waterfall and climbed up the rocks at the side, as if she were used to doing it, and she stood on the shaky little bridge at the top with 'the-king-of-the-castle' air that was very irritating. She smiled amiably down at me, and called, "You can't reach me up here!"

"I don't want to," I called back. "Because I know it's dangerous. I'd come down, if I were you, before that bridge breaks and you fall."

She shook her head. "You're only saying that, because you don't like me. But I've got a secret. I could tell you, if I wanted to."

I watched the bridge, and assessed the chances of it holding under my weight, while I tried to get hers off it. I didn't rate the chances as very high. Even as I watched, the bridge gave a little lurch under her dancing steps. "Look out, it's breaking away!" I called, but she only laughed and shouted, "Don't be silly. My fella said it would he all right, and he wouldn't say that if it wasn't."

I looked sharply up. "Your fella? You mean . . . you can't mean Mr Darrell?" I couldn't help it, I was just incredulous, since the last time I had seen them together, she had injured him in her temper, so that the blood had been trickling down his cheek.

"That's right," she laughed. "He likes me. I gave him a lot of my pretty things to go and sell, and he's coming back for me. He's going to take me away, you know."

I couldn't believe it. Much more likely that Darrell had persuaded her to part with her things and she would never see him again.

"What sort of pretty things?" I asked, as I began to climb the rocks at the side of the waterfall.

"My jewellery. Heywood gives me a lot of jewellery, you know."

"Oh, for birthdays," I said, keeping her talking.

"Birthdays and Christmas and anniversaries and every Saturday and things," she said, reeling them off in the sing-song voice of a child.

I was more than half way up. I didn't know what I was going to do but I had to get up there before that bridge gave way; I couldn't think why Heywood didn't have it either repaired or taken away altogether. I said, "I suppose you're hiding from Darrell, then?"

"Of course not! He told me to come here and stand on the middle of the bridge and wait for him, where he could see me, and," she added proudly, "he told me to wear a green dress and a green scarf over my hair so that nobody would see me while I was going through the woods. Isn't he clever?"

Too clever, I thought bitterly. Had Darrell merely given her those complicated instructions to keep her busy and happy, or had he really been trying to kill her, and making it look like an accident?

"Didn't he know the bridge wasn't safe, Aurelia? Didn't he think you would fall?" I asked, desperately making a final effort and reaching the top.

"It isn't unsafe," she said, surprise lighting her face. "Look, come on it and I'll prove it," and she began to dance up and down, and the old wood creaked ominously and lurched.

My heart was in my mouth. I didn't know what to do for the best. If she wasn't careful, she would have the pair of us down. The pool at the bottom looked, for the first time, a dizzying long way down.

And then quite suddenly things happened and it was all over. Heywood's voice came, like the crack of a whip, from down below. "Get off that bridge, Emma!"

Aurelia stopped smiling and looked at him, backing fearfully away. She backed into the arms of Hilda, who slapped a pad over her mouth and nose and held it there. I backed off my end of the little bridge, Hilda lifted Aurelia bodily off her end, limp as a rag, like a rag-doll hanging over her arm, having presumably been chloroformed. And as we moved in reverse directions simultaneously, the little bridge gave an ominous crack and collapsed. Like matchwood, it fell in pieces to the sparkling water of the pool below. The bits of wood were tossed about like flotsam before they sank, but the waterfall kept on and on falling, down that dreadful depth, with a horrid sort of inevitability.

Heywood shouted, "Don't look down. I'm coming up for you. Don't worry, Hilda's got Aurelia."

She had. She was climbing easily down the rocks on the other side, the girl slung over her shoulder. Now I saw the children down there, watching eagerly as Heywood climbed up for me.

He reached the top and stood there. "We'd better go down the back through the woods. I have things to say to you." I nodded, and we turned and went. I thought I knew what he was going to say.

But I was wrong. Once over the hump and down into the woods, out of sight of the children, he stopped, and took me into his arms, in an almost savage gesture, and I felt the hardness of his body and could hear the strong thumping of his heart.

"Will you never learn," he hissed into my ear, "to keep that inquisitive little nose of yours out of things? Don't you realize, you might have been thrown off that bridge as it collapsed? You might have been dead by now!"

7

HIS action took me absolutely by surprise. I couldn't move or think or say anything. The woods that arched above my head spun round in a dizzy mess of darkening leaves, for the light was going out of the day now. So much had happened this day, and here was I held tight in Heywood's arms. The sensation was even more upsetting than it had been before, and it was nothing like that earlier experience, when he had comforted me in my grief for poor old Colin Ketwill.

I pulled myself together. This simply wouldn't do. I pushed out of his arms, and I said, "What would have happened if I hadn't been inquisitive? She would have fallen to her death and nobody would have known!"

"I think not!" he retorted, digging his hands into his pockets, and no doubt very sorry for that exhibition of his. "I imagine she knew perfectly well that you were following her and she just climbed to the top to shock you. She does that sort of thing. It's always best not to appear worried or impressed by the things she does."

"I'm learning." I said bitterly. "Next time I'll go the other way."

"There won't be a next time," he said shortly, "because I intend to get from you how Aurelia came to be in the woods, before we return to the house."

So that was it. He wasn't really concerned for my safety. He had just been blowing off steam, and now he wanted to know what part Darrell had played in that scene up in the roof apartment this afternoon. I said shortly, "How do I know, Mr Stanton? I was with you, on the shore, remember? Why don't you ask the people who *were* concerned? Hilda, for instance, who seems to be always missing when she's wanted."

That stung him. "Don't you decry the services of Hilda," he said, in a dangerously quiet tone. "I don't honestly know what I'd do without her and she has to have time off sometimes. What I want to know is how my half-brother got to the island. I suppose he came back with you. And since you were told not to leave the island — "

"You know I came back alone," I stormed. "And you know why I went to the mainland — because you won't have a telephone on the island. Poor old Mr Ketwill *said* something would happen that would make you sorry for cutting off the telephone!" I blurted out.

It was a mistake, of course. "Did he indeed," he said. "And I suppose I may infer from that bit of slipped information that you told him everything you had discovered about my private business."

"No, I didn't, and that's not fair. You must know perfectly well that I wouldn't do that. The fact is, I was looking for a telephone booth and he asked why I didn't wait until I had got back to the island to telephone in peace and privacy, and it was natural to say there was no phone out here."

"Oh. I see." He strode on beside me, his mouth a hard uncompromising line. Then he suddenly changed that grim mood. "I'm sorry, Emma. I do growl at you, don't I? If you weren't here I don't know who I'd fly at in my temper. You'll be glad when your holiday comes to an end, won't you?"

I wouldn't. I didn't want my holiday

to end. I couldn't hear the thought of leaving the island now, because of him. But I wasn't going to say so. "I can't wait for my holidays to end!" I flared at him, and he was in such a state that he believed me. I could see he believed me, and I was so furious that I wouldn't retract that statement. No, I had to go further, amplify it. "And what is more, if I'm inquisitive, it's only because I like helping people, and because I'm open and frank by nature, and ever since I've come to the island I've been aware of things going on under the surface, secrets. Oh, I know they are none of my business, but it would have been easier for me if you'd just said that you had an old patient in the roof apartment and didn't want the children to go up there. It would have been easier if you'd have warned me that there's a man on the island who has an odious boy who is supposed to be allowed to smash up the children's boat and nothing is to be said to him. It would have been easier if you'd told me that Mrs Boyd was your mother, and that you'd got a half brother who was likely to sneak out here. All these things would have at least warned me of what to expect. As it is — "

"Well?" he said, his voice like ice. "As it is — ?"

"As it is, I don't know how many other unpleasant things will happen to jolt me out of trying to enjoy my so-called holiday on the island, and the job that goes with it," I snapped back.

Well, I suppose it blew off steam, so there was some good in all that, but it was a pity. It drove us further apart, so that he was tempted to give me a lecture on minding my own business and doing the job I undertook to do, the job that suited my convenience until I could go to be a nurse, and he succumbed to the temptation and let his tongue lash me like a whip. When we reached the house, I think it's fair to say that we were loathing each other pretty thoroughly, and both of us were rather unhappy.

No use saying I should have known better, I suppose, because I'd had one or two shocks that day and I was still in the throes of my unhappy discovery that I was in love with him. And I'm quite sure it would have been no use blaming it all on to Heywood. He had his troubles, too many of them, and I'm pretty sure he didn't mean that half an hour to end like that.

My day wasn't finished, by any means. The children rounded on me for being a party to the new rule that they couldn't leave the island. "What on earth can we do here?" they demanded. "It's dull! And you were going to take us to Poltoncross. You promised!"

"What's the attraction about Poltoncross?" I asked coldly. "The Public Library, or Darrell Boyd?"

They all looked shifty, and red in the face, and admitted to a bit of both.

"I thought so. Like everyone else, nobody tells me the things I should know," I told them heatedly. "All right, so you can't go on the mainland. Well, how about us really exploring the island? Couldn't it be fun? We did get on well together, and nothing's changed really, has it?"

"Except that that old man died," Jenneth said, staring, "and you kept crying and Heywood Stanton cuddled you, after you said you hated him like we did," and she made a sick noise to show her disgust at my perfidy.

"And you apparently were a Peeping Tom," I reminded her sharply. "Yes, I was crying. I liked the old man. It was a shock to find that he had got ill of his heart again, and had died. To be honest, anyone would have suited me just then, to give me a shoulder to cry on. When you grow up, you might find that things just get too much, and you feel you'd like someone to lean on for just a little while. Well, that's the way I felt. But I don't any more, if it's any comfort to you all. I'm pretty fed-up with Mr Stanton, especially as I've got into trouble for being mixed up in things you three could have warned me about, like Mr Darrell Boyd, for instance and why the Macey boy bashes your boat every so often, and that girl on the roof."

They looked pretty ashamed, so I thought it was time I called a truce, and by the time their bedtime arrived, we were all friends again.

Well, friends. I suppose one could say that, but it didn't mean that they had felt it necessary to give me their entire confidence, although I didn't know that then. I found that out later, to my cost. But they *looked* as if we were all friends again and that they liked me. Timmy leaned on me, as he had always done, and Jenneth stopped looking so sharp and adult. And I, like a fool, thought it was all right.

I had other things on my mind, anyway. I had just seen the children to bed, when I was sent for. Mary Abbott was serving the evening meal, and she said that Mr Stanton and his mother wanted me to eat with them. She also advised me to put on something decent if I had anything, because there was a visitor.

Very much puzzled, because this sort of thing had not happened so far, and on an evening when Heywood and I had been at each other's throats, it was even more unlikely, I hesitated.

"*Have* you got anything decent?" Mary Abbott asked bluntly. And as I shot my head up in anger at her tone, she said, "Look, miss, it's nothing to do with me, but I happen to know that the visitor is a lawyer from London and Mrs Boyd and her son are all excited. I don't know what's up, but if it was me in your shoes, I'd want to look decent. That's all I can say."

So, I told myself bitterly, she, too, had been listening at doors. She knew something. Everyone else here but me could get away with eavesdropping, but not me. Oh, no, even the most accidental eavesdropping on my part, and Heywood was at me, accusing me of being inquisitive.

So I got out my best dress, a soft dark blue, and my light blue sandals, and I wore the one good thing I had round my neck — a fine gold chain with a frail pendant on the end of it. At least I wasn't going to make the mistake of wearing artificial pearls.

But you can't do much with a short, business-like hair cut and my hair was absolutely straight. The straight fringe looked so childish. I tried brushing it back but it jumped away, into the old set as if it were alive and as obstinate as I was. So I gave it up. I looked clean-scrubbed, an orphan in her Sunday best, I told myself in derision.

Heywood stared when I knocked on the door and was told to enter. They were in the big drawing-room. The visitor was standing, in dinner jacket and bow tie, looking elegant in a slightly old-fashioned way, a glass in his hand, and he stared, too. Mrs Boyd rose slowly, looking at me with an odd expression, but I had eyes for nobody but Heywood. He was so tall and handsome in a lean, hungry sort of way, and he looked so marvellous dressed for dinner. I went on staring so he put his glass down and came over and took my hand, leading me back to the fireplace.

"This is Emma," he said quietly, in a sort of special voice, as if he were introducing the girl he loved, the girl he was going to marry. I looked rather dazed, but almost at once I was enlightened as to what I felt was the reason for his old-world courtesy.

"Ah," said Mr Fawdry, the lawyer, "so this is the heiress. Have they told you, my dear, that you have inherited near on a quarter of a million?"

I suppose I looked pretty blank. "From Mr Ketwill," Mrs Boyd said, as if it hurt her to say it. "We always thought he would leave some of his money to poor Heywood, who has this big house to keep up, but apparently he took a fancy to you, my dear, and left you everything."

I sat down, because my legs wouldn't hold me up. I hadn't even known that Colin Ketwill was as rich as that. Comfortably off, perhaps, but not so madly rich. And all I could think of was the chauffeur, too choked to speak to me over the telephone. Too grief-filled at the loss of a beloved master. I voiced my thoughts aloud. "Then I shall keep the Rolls," I said, "and the chauffeur."

Distaste filled their faces. I didn't think of it then but I suppose it sounded as if I was getting uppish already. I made no attempt to explain. I couldn't have done. I was only thankful that I could do something for poor Mr Ketwill's faithful servant, though I don't really think I saw myself going out in the Rolls in style. Perhaps taking the children out in it for a picnic, as Colin Ketwill had taken us, many times. And perhaps asking the chauffeur to drive me to one of those places where Colin Ketwill had taken me to tea, and talked. It had been the first time that I had had anyone to confide in, with any hope of my confidences being kept secret. And he had given me such good advice about life. But why had he left all that much money to *me?*

I don't remember much of that evening. I was treated as the guest of honour, and afterwards I had to go into the library with

218

the lawyer while he discussed investments and went over long, long lists of dreary figures. There were three estates, and I had to make up my mind whether to sell them or not. I began to wish Colin Ketwill had left all his money to Heywood. Much better for him to have to make all these decisions.

They told me I should have to go to the funeral. "He had nobody else," the lawyer said. I agreed, if Heywood Stanton would go with me, and his mother, and the lawyer, but his mother said she must stay on the island to keep an eye on things, which meant, I suppose, that she wanted Darrell there with her, and she had to keep an eye on the children in my absence.

The following week was like a bad dream. Heywood was different to me. Polite, as he would be to a stranger, a wealthy stranger who could do as she pleased, and already he was asking me diffidently what my plans were and when I thought I was going to leave the island.

I stared at him, open-mouthed. I was still wretched about the funeral. It had been such a stark and lonely affair. A rich old man, with only his heiress, his lawyer, and one other person to follow him on that last ride. I remembered him as I had first seen him, fighting for breath, on the end of the half finished promenade at Chighampton. He had loved life, and now he was gone, and his wealth was going to drive me out from Moon Island.

I said, rather stupidly, it seemed to me, "Do I have to go?"

"Well, I don't imagine you will want to stay here on the pittance my mother gives you, and act as nursemaid to those brats, will you?" Heywood said harshly.

"Why not?" I said, reasonably. "Nothing's changed. I'm still going to the hospital to train as a nurse."

"Don't be so stupid!" he snapped. "After all the publicity that my mother has steered you through, do you think you will be welcome at the hospital? Well, what do you think they will think of you? They'll think you're playing at the thing, or hogging publicity, even if Matron doesn't say outright that it would be frankly upsetting in the P.T.S. to have a trainee who was a rich young woman who had no need to work and had been in all the newspapers."

I sat down on a rock. He had caught me up as I had been walking along one of those stark beaches, rockstrewn, beyond sight of the house, which I loved so much. Here one could feel at the end of the world. I wanted time to think and he was trying to hustle me off the island.

"Do you mean to say that I can't go back to St John's to be a nurse?"

"Use your sense, Emma," he begged me, forgetting his polite cool manner to the heiress. "Of course you can't, but you shouldn't want to!"

"What else is there for me to do?" I asked blankly. "I've never wanted anything else."

"Well, that's only because you saw it as a job with a roof over your head and security. All girls on their own look at a job in that light. You would have felt taken care of, with the weight of Matron and the nursing staff behind you. But it's different now. With all that money, well, the world is your oyster."

"But what would I do with it? There's the car and the chauffeur and I must take care of him — "

"Take care of him! That's a funny way

of looking at employing a man to drive and look after your Rolls."

I looked helplessly at him. I couldn't explain. And I think in that moment he understood my remark about the Rolls and the chauffeur.

He softened a little, and came and sat on the rock, with an arm loosely around my shoulders. "You're such a child, Emma. Such a wilful, obstinate, sensible yet daft, child. Such an adorable child, too. Don't stay here, my dear, or we'll spoil you. We're so selfishly caught up in our own problems, before you know where you are, you'll find yourself the general factotum again, and that will be dreadful."

"Why will it? At least I'll be wanted, and I shall be doing the things I like. If you make me leave here, where can I go? Not to a hotel in Chighampton like Mr Ketwill. I wouldn't like that."

"You could open up one or other of the estates," Heywood said, with a half smile. "You could amuse yourself with engaging servants, and redecorating the place — I'm sure it would need it."

"But what for? To live on my own?"

"There would be no dearth of friends,

Emma. Once you start entertaining, you will wonder why you were never so popular before."

"I wouldn't want that sort of popularity," I said bleakly.

"No, I don't suppose you would. But my dear, there's a formula for the way of living, with big money. You ought to be launched into it. My mother would do it for you, and do it well, only I don't want her to." He looked frosty again, and when I asked why, he said at once, "You should know. My half brother, who eats money, would be on your back at once."

"It would be a problem for him to eat his way through a quarter of a million, wouldn't it?" I smiled. Not because I liked Darrell Boyd, but because it somehow hurt me to see Heywood hating him so much. It grieved his mother, too, I knew.

"Just don't give him the chance to get started on it," Heywood said, getting up. "And now, my child, I'm asking you again — when are you leaving the island?"

I jumped up, angry again. "I'm not going. I want to stay here. Can't you see? This is still my holiday, but it's more than that.

I know you and your mother, and the children. It's got into a sort of family situation. It's my security. Well, at least let me keep it until I get used to the new state of things," I pleaded, and with that, he agreed.

His face twisted into a lopsided smile. "You're an odd child," he commented. "I would have thought you'd be dashing off to the shops to buy things. Don't you realize — you can have anything you want now! There's no limit!"

"But I don't *want* anything," I said reasonably, "except a few coins to give the children sometimes, for sweets and ice-cream."

His face closed. "Oh, yes, I'm glad you reminded me. They let that out — they had no business to take money from you. They have money of their own. They should have come to me."

I laughed. "Oh, now you're being silly! Children don't stop to question which member of the family gives them money when they want to buy something. The adult with them will do very well, and I am the adult with them most of the time."

"Then I will give you money for the

purpose," he said coldly.

"Oh, don't be like that with me," I murmured, not really meaning to say it. It just popped out.

"What do you mean?" he asked sharply.

I turned away, embarrassed. If anyone ever wore her heart on her sleeve, it was me. I said, trying to get out of it gracefully, "Sometimes you're so friendly, and I forget I'm an orphan. You don't have to be so cold and distant with me, do you? What have I done to you?"

He looked at me, and I almost read his thoughts. What had I done? I had dazzled an old man to the extent of leaving his fortune where it wasn't wanted, when Heywood needed money so badly and had been led to expect some from that quarter.

"You must forgive me if I snap, Emma, but I have my problems," he said.

"I know, and if only I could give away all this money, I would," I said. "But I don't know who to give it away to." And my whole heart wanted to give it to him, but even I wasn't such a fool as to suggest it. At least I must leave him his pride.

Anyway, the idea had nothing to offer

to him, it seemed. "Don't be absurd, Emma," he requested me. "If it worries you, the thought of being so rich, just remember that the legal wallahs will do all the business for you. And remember, too, that poor old Ketwill wanted to leave it to you. He wasn't forced to. A man can leave his possessions to whom he likes, when he has no further use for them."

"But I must put them to good use," I fretted. "What would *you* have done, if you'd been left a lot of money like this?"

"It doesn't apply. My problems aren't the same," he said, stiffly.

"I suppose you would have had Moon House made strong and good again," I said. "It's such a nice house." I glanced at him and he winced, so I hastily thought of something less touchy to mention. "And I suppose you could afford to have the waterfall taken away. It really is an eyesore, isn't it?"

"You think so, too?" he asked, and for an instant, we were one again. "No, nobody can take it away. It isn't so easy to change the path of water."

"I don't understand! You said with all that much money, anything was possible."

"Except interfering with nature," he said harshly. "It was made a long time ago, and since then the cliffs in Valerian's Bay have eroded and the tide rushes in with a much greater force."

"But what's that to do with the waterfall?" I asked blankly.

"Do you know anything about engineering, Emma? Dam-making? Flooding and turning the tide of rivers and sea-power? Then why ask a silly question like that? I can't give you a potted explanation. I'm not really too certain of it myself. I only know that an engineer we once had staying here looked very anxiously at the thing and remarked that some rich men can be rather foolish, the way they try to change natural things."

"Well, what if the rocks making the waterfall were knocked down? Or built up, so that the water could be turned back into the sea?"

"It's done by an arrangement of the rocks," he said, at last. "It's quite primitive, I understand. It was done in the East way back in Bible days. But once you start the thing, it can't be stopped without disaster."

"What sort of disaster?" I asked, still not understanding.

"Perhaps you wouldn't consider flooding the whole island a disaster?"

That terminated our scintillating conversation for that day. I went to find the children, in a far from happy frame of mind, and it wasn't them that I found, but Darrell Boyd. The children had told me that his name meant 'the beloved' and I remembered how his mother looked at him. He was the favourite of her two sons. Why, I wondered? Because he was weak, and likely to get into trouble? Or because he needed her most? Perhaps that was it. Heywood was so self-sufficient. He liked to battle with his own problems — he just didn't want help.

Darrell Boyd stood square in my path and said, "Well, well, well, Emma — well-met, my dear. So now we are an heiress, and not attached to anyone."

I watched him warily. I didn't like the way he chose his words, as if he were laughing at me.

"Lost your tongue, my dear? Come now, still wearing the same faded dress and old espadrilles? What can my mother be thinking about? She should have taken you to London, or to Paris — no, Milan. Italian fashions nowadays would be just the thing for that *gamin* personality of yours. What's wrong? Won't they let you get at all that lovely lolly yet?"

"I've not changed, Mr Boyd."

"Darrell," he corrected. "Let's be friends, Emma, now you're no longer the little dogsbody around here."

"Oh, but I am." I informed him. "I just told you — I've not changed. I don't even know if I'm going to accept all that money. In fact, if I could only find out some charity which Mr Ketwill had the slightest interest in, I would give it all to them at once."

He looked really alarmed. "I say, don't be so stupid," he begged me. "Some of it, if your conscience troubles you so much, but for heaven's sake keep some for the needy around you. Well, poor old Heywood, for instance."

"He wouldn't want anyone's charity," I said quickly. "He likes to settle his own problems."

"So he says," Darrell almost sneered. "But do you think he'd hesitate if he had enough to settle Aurelia in a cosy nursing-home with enough people detailed to keep her busy and happy? Do you think he really likes hiding out in this hole? You haven't seen it in the winter, my love, and my poor mother would jump at the chance of going back to the South of France or Capri — she's crippled with rheumatism in the winter months."

"Is she? I didn't know that," I gasped. But of course, I had heard the wistful note in her voice when she had told me about the times when she had lived in the sun.

"It takes money to get someone like Aurelia put comfortably out of harm's way, and believe me, it would be good for everyone. That girl could really do someone a mischief, if they caught her in the wrong mood. Poor old Hilda would like to be released, too. Life isn't too hot for her."

"But how would one persuade a proud person like your half-brother to accept so much money?" I murmured. After all, it was my interest, too.

"Oh, that's easy," Darrell said. "But of course, if I told you the way, I'd want compensating."

"You'd get your compensation," I said impatiently. "How could I give big money to Heywood?"

I wasted a lot of time haggling with him but at last, after I had given him a sizeable cheque, he told me. "It's fool proof. You just approach his bank manager and say that you want to give your friend Heywood a surprise and it's to be a secret and to inform Heywood that some of his shares have leapt up. Simple."

I was furious. "It's a swindle! Do you think for a moment that Heywood wouldn't rush to the newspaper to see by how much they'd jumped and to work it out himself! Give me that cheque back — you've cheated me!"

"I know, love," he chuckled, holding it out of reach. "Let that be your first valuable lesson in dodging con men, of whom there will be plenty. I deserve this hundred quid just for my kindness in giving you such a lesson."

"I shall stop payment of that cheque," I said.

"No, you won't," he said confidently, tucking it away. "Because you like my mother and you wouldn't want her to be hurt and ashamed — as she would be, of course."

Well, that was the only money he would get out of me, I told myself angrily. It wasn't that I couldn't afford such a loss. It was the principle of the thing. He had made me feel so naive, such an easy fool. What was worse, I knew he'd always be thinking up fresh ideas to get money out of me.

After that episode, it was a relief to go and find the children. "Do you know I've got a lot of money?" I asked them.

"Yes, and we know how much," Jenneth said smartly.

"Are you going to let it make any difference?" I demanded, but I looked at Sheldon, not the little ones.

"You mean you're going to stay here? Just as before?" He couldn't believe it.

"Yes, I'm going to stay here as if nothing had happened — except, of course, that the Rolls is now mine, and I'm going to get permission for us all to go trips on the mainland in it."

They considered that, and then Sheldon said, with a wisdom beyond his years, "But it can't go on as before, Emma. I don't know why, I just know it can't be the same as before, because it isn't the same. You think you can make it the same because you haven't got used to being rich. But you will."

I gazed at him helplessly. I felt near tears, it was so awful for such a young boy to be so worldly-wise.

"I didn't think that out for myself," he had the grace to admit. "I overheard the grown-ups talking (Cripley and Mary Abbott actually) but it sort of makes sense. You must see that, Emma."

I smiled through my tears. "Well, I'm glad it wasn't your idea, Sheldon. I couldn't imagine you'd sprouted into such a worldly-wise horror overnight. Oh, come on, let's go swimming. Let's have some fun, for once."

While we were playing around in the water, the helicopter went over, and people stared down at us. And a pleasure boat came out from Chighampton and loitered near, and the people on board all had field glasses and telescopes and stared at the island. It was me, now, of course, exciting their curiosity, but Heywood would be so angry. I looked uncomfortably at the children, but they weren't thinking about the money any more. They were being children, happy, playing at porpoises, diving in and out of the water as if they lived in it. I thanked heaven for the children, momentarily. But there would still be Heywood's wrath to face.

Perhaps because things were moving up too quickly on me, made me suggest doing things, anything, for new fun. And into my mind popped the thought of Black Valerian's cave. "You know," I said, mentioning it to Sheldon, "I would rather like to see it. Are you sure it's impossible to get into it?"

"No, you can get into it, but we're not supposed to. I'm game, but what about the little ones?"

"We're not little!" Jenneth shouted.

"You are when it comes to safety," Sheldon said, with rare big-brotherly care.

"Well, let's have a look at it from the outside," I said. I wasn't consciously tempting them to do wrong. I was so sure that I could keep them from danger myself.

They, of course, didn't need any second bidding. We got out and dried and put on the shirts, shorts and beach shoes we had been wearing, and rushed round the island until we had to make the climb up to the cave.

It really was an exhausting climb, and then there was a rather dangerous narrow staircase down the cliff face. I looked doubtfully at it, but of course, having come so far, the children weren't going to be put off. But they were so sure-footed with their climbing, I thought, remembering that first time I had made friends with them through the climb up the cliffs, that surely no harm could come of it?

We got down to the cave mouth without much difficulty. It looked quite innocuous, too. Much too innocent to be boarded up. But the sea had already almost rotted the slatted gate away, and it fell almost at a touch. That should have told me. It would take great sea power to batter at such a gate as this must have once been.

However, we went in. "We need torches," I said doubtfully, for the cave turned sharply and was lost in inky blackness.

Sheldon grinned. "I'll get you some lights. Actually we stored some near here for an expedition on the last day of the holidays. I mean, we'd have gone back to school before anyone found out, and then it wouldn't be worth while saying anything to us."

He had a cache of candles, matches, torches and batteries, in a tin box, sunk in dry sand. He was proud of his planning, but a little nervous, I thought.

"Shouldn't we have left a message somewhere?" Jenneth asked, doubtfully. "Like they do in books."

Sheldon appeared to think. "Yes! But not you, Jenneth — give Timmy a chance to take the message and we'll wait for him."

Timmy swelled with pride. He took the written slip which he was to give to Oliver Cripley to deliver to the house while he ran back to us. But the minute Timmy had gone, Sheldon said, "Now, we three will go, and we'll shut the gate behind us. That note asks the person to hang on to Timmy. He's too small," and he went on calmly paying out line and giving us the ends to tie round our middles. I began to feel I shouldn't have suggested this expedition.

But it was exciting, once we were in the cave. Our lights picked out the fascinating interior, and I wanted to stay and look at some strange markings high on the walls, but Sheldon wouldn't let me. "We don't want to be caught by the tide, do we? We have to find the exit. It's high up."

It took us an hour of slow walking through two feet of water. There was a ledge in places, but it wandered high until it almost touched the roof. There were old kegs and metal bound trunks which Jenneth said was pirate treasure and wanted to stop to break them open but Sheldon made us press on.

He fascinated me. Sometimes he was just a naughty adventurous boy, and at others he was a knowledgeable being on the verge of being mentally adult.

I said, "Do you know how the waterfall works, Sheldon?"

He stopped. "What made you ask that?" he demanded, and I fancied there was fear in his voice.

"I just wondered. I did ask Mr Stanton but he said he couldn't explain in simple terms and if I didn't understand water engineering it was no good."

Sheldon shrugged. "I've just thought of it. There's a deep place that always has water in it when the tide goes out. It was dug out and cemented to catch the tide, like permanent swimming pools on the shore for the kids, you know what I mean. Only this is very deep indeed. It makes an awful lot of weight of water, to force it to the top of the waterfall, then when it drops into the pool, it goes through a big pipe just like those that empty swimming baths, only something happened and it got a lot more suction than they did, and that's why it's dangerous. But it makes a marvellous waterfall and it's all done by sea power."

"I think it's horrible. Where is this dug-out place?"

"Just below this cave, of course," Sheldon said. "But you knew that, didn't you? Wasn't that why you wanted to come — to see the water rush in and disappear?"

"No!" I gasped, shocked. "At least, I thought it was just a smuggler's cave, not a natural feed for the waterfall. What time is high tide?"

He told me, looking at his watch. "It's all right, we've got half an hour to get to the high ground at the top."

Jenneth asked him what he made the time. When he told her, she said, her face whitening to the lips, "I think your watch has stopped, Sheldon. It's high tide any minute now."

We all stood and looked at each other for a wretched stunned minute. I looked around to see where we could climb higher, but Sheldon shouted at me, something I didn't hear, because of a terrible growling and booming. Then he leapt over to where I stood and lifted my wrist and checked the time by my watch. "She's right," he yelled. "Here comes the water — run, everybody!"

I couldn't run. The others did. Sheldon pulled his sister up to the ledge, and their movement tugged at the rope round my waist. I was listening and it seemed as if great monsters were coming behind us, with the speed of light. No, not quite like that — it was like waiting for an express train to roar out of a tunnel, with the same explosive power. The rope round my waist tightened, then slackened. But the thing I noticed most was a curious slap right in the middle of my back, and I was lifted and thrown, high up on to the ledge. Then I was sucked almost off it, but the rope round me was tightening again. It held, and the water fell back and found its own level, but I couldn't see. The last thing I really remembered was a bang on the back of my head and I must have blacked out.

8

MY head was throbbing dully when I came to. Jenneth was kneeling over me, unashamedly crying, and slopping salt water all over my face.

The salt hurt my eyes, but it made me sit up sharply protesting. A thousand knives stabbed my head and I felt sick and lay back again.

"Don't, Jen," I heard Sheldon say. "That's enough. She's come round." He looked anxiously down at me. "I say, are you all right, Emma? I'm awfully sorry. We must have done it, pulling on the rope, only you wouldn't move."

"What did you do?" I asked him.

"Well, sort of tugged you off your feet, I suppose, and the tide-race caught you in the back and swept you up here. We are all right at the moment, but how are we going to get you out?"

"I'll try and get up," I said.

I hurt all over, but especially one ankle. "I think it's a sprain."

241

We all examined it with clinical interest. It was swelling fast. "Well, you can't walk on that," Sheldon said, with finality. "The going's rough. We went to have a look."

"Not together," Jenneth said quickly, as I looked alarmed. "One of us stayed with you to keep watch in case you fell off the ledge into the water."

"Oh, good," I said weakly, trying to laugh. "I wouldn't have liked that."

"You're a sport," Jenneth said warmly. "We thought you'd be livid."

"How could I be? It was my fault — I shouldn't have suggested this trip. What a thing to have happened. Mr Stanton is the one who'll be livid."

"Well, it's all right for you. You don't have to stay. With all your money, you could buy his old island off him and make a rude noise and go off and leave him — or turn him out," she added for good measure.

So that was how they felt about him.

"There's a saying," I ventured, eyeing her thoughtfully, "that possession is nine points of the law. That means who owns it doesn't have to sell if he doesn't want to, no matter how many fortunes anyone else has got."

She was really dismayed. "Oh, I thought you'd be able to boss *him* right now, Emma. Well, what's the use of all that money, then?"

What, indeed? Not that I wanted to boss him but I did so much want to help him, although I hadn't really had much hope that he would let me.

I tried standing, but it was too hazardous. In the end, I crawled along the ledge on hands and knees, Jenneth leading the way, Sheldon behind me in case I slipped. Heavens, I was the adult who was supposed to be looking after them, and they were looking after me! What would Heywood say?

It was a long and painful journey. The tide had turned and was fast running out before we got to the top. My face was filthy, and wet with perspiration. I was worn out with the effort, but we had reached the place where the daylight filtered in.

I sank back, intending to rest, but the children looked so horrified, I sat up again. "What's wrong?" I gasped.

Sheldon went forward to look at

something and Jenneth looked very scared. I said, "Jen, what's wrong? Tell me!"

"There was a place big enough to crawl out but it seems to have gone."

"Gone? But how could it? When did you see it last?"

"Just before you came to," she said.

Sheldon came back. "A big stone has been rolled over the hole," he said.

And then someone laughed, a horrid tinkly laugh. I got up and crawled on all fours towards it. There were small places where daylight was coming in. Through one of them I could see Aurelia's face, and she was the one who was laughing. "You can't get out now," she said.

I looked at Sheldon. "*Could* she roll a big stone over the hole?"

"Well, yes, it's not hard, up there. It's hard for us to roll it back because we'd have to have an extra pair of hands," he scowled. "We'll need both hands to climb up there even if the stone wasn't there."

"Then I'll have to talk to her," I said, but she had gone away.

Timmy was there. "I can't move it. It's too big for me," he said. He was crying. Sheldon shouted. "Don't be a baby,

Timmy. Shut up and listen to me. Who did you give the note to?"

"I didn't. She saw it and she made me give it to her," he sobbed.

"Oh, *no*," I murmured. "There's only one thing, then. *Timmy!*" I shouted. "Where is she now? Can she see you?"

"Yes. She's dancing round the trees," he offered.

"Somehow you've got to run back and find Mr Stanton and you mustn't let her catch you. Do you understand?"

He said he did, and he'd try, but I hadn't much hope. How could you assess what a fey thing like Aurelia would do? What could she do to Timmy?

Jenneth said, "It'll take hours. Can't *we* do something, Sheldon?"

He was poking around, and found a length of driftwood. "If this doesn't break, and if she isn't watching, I might shift it."

Then followed a horrible half hour. It felt ten times as long. My head hurt and my foot was swollen and painful. Every bone in my body felt bruised. I think I went to sleep sometimes, or blacked out. I know I wasn't any help at all to Sheldon and Jenneth. They must have worked like two adults, for suddenly I heard Sheldon shout. There was a rush and a roar, and he threw his sister back on to me, and collapsed on us both himself. It was the only place, at short notice, that he could think of in order to avoid the great fall of stones and rocks. But there was a way out, although we must climb over a pile of rough stones to reach it.

And then Heywood's head appeared in the hole.

I saw Timmy's head bob up near, and someone pulled him back. There were other people there — Oliver Cripley, and the wretched Macey man. But I couldn't take my eyes off Heywood. He looked terrible, like a man who has been very ill, or just had a bad shock. Oh, I wouldn't hear the last of this, I thought! He must have thought that both Jenneth and Sheldon had been drowned. They were in his charge. It must have been terrible news for him.

It never occurred to me at that moment that he was worried about me. He climbed down and scooped me up in his arms, as if the children didn't exist. Cripley and the others helped them up.

Heywood stormed back to the house, carrying me. People spoke to him but he didn't answer. He stared at his poor mother as if she were a stranger and requested her to get out of the way. He was like a man possessed. He took me straight up to my room and laid me on the bed, and bent over me, taking in every detail of my face, and then, pulling himself together, he muttered, "Must examine you — see if there are any broken bones."

I felt the colour rushing to my face. "No!" I said. I couldn't have Heywood examine me. I said, "There's only my ankle troubling me — nothing else. Strap that up if you like but don't you touch me!"

He was appalled. "Are you afraid I might hurt you?" he gasped.

I didn't know where to look. "No, I *know* you wouldn't," I said on a low note. And then somehow he caught on, what I meant, and I caught on that he didn't hate me, as I'd thought, and somehow we sort of merged together and he held me to him in a grip that hurt, and he feverishly kissed me, all over my dirty face, and one hand pushed back my hair, which must have looked the untidiest, wettest mess on earth, and in between kissing me, he said things; personal things to us, that I knew I would treasure for ever, whatever the outcome might be.

Not that his remarks were very coherent or that I was in any state to take them in really. Only one thing he said made any sense, and that thing he kept saying over and over again: "Oh, Emma, I thought I'd lost you!"

At last his mother came in. "This is all very fine, Heywood, but the child is safe, so do let me make her comfortable. She needs a hot bath and putting to bed, and bless me, look at that ankle. If you're not going to attend to it, then I shall have to!"

Heywood said he would do it, after I'd been put to bed. Then he stood looking down at me, smoothing his hair, and smiling a little, ruefully. "Made an ass of myself, did I?" he murmured, as he bent over me again.

"No, behaved like a human being for once," I retorted.

"That's my Emma," he said, straightening up and laughing. "Smile all over your face and make a remark with a kick like a mule. Still, I've got your measure, young woman," and he went away to leave me to his mother's ministrations.

She said wryly, as she helped me into the bath, "He nearly went out of his mind when he heard there had been a cave-in, and that you were there. I don't think he realized that Sheldon and Jenneth were with you. I expect those two will get the rough edge of his tongue, when be remembers."

"Oh, don't let that happen," I pleaded. "It was my fault. I wanted to see the cave and I made them take me."

"I don't suppose they needed much making," she said, as she washed my hair and put the dryer on it. "How do you feel now, child? Foot hurts?"

"Well, yes, but I'll survive. I'm bruised all over, aren't I?"

"You are indeed," she said, and smiled. "Bored with your fortune already, I suppose. Frankly I'd have felt happier if you'd gone to London shopping. It would have been more natural."

"Not for me," I said, suppressing a yawn. "Oh, it's been an exciting day. That reminds me. What happened to Aurelia and how did she get out? She was the one who rolled the stone over the escape hole, you know."

Her face closed, and I guessed. I said, "Oh, it will be your son Darrell's work. He lets her out. You knew, didn't you?"

She nodded, and supporting me deftly, off my bad foot, she wrapped a big fluffy bath robe round me. "Emma, you're going to be imposed on. By us, you know," she said, and helped me back into the bedroom.

"No, never. I feel as if you are all my family," I said, with a degree of silly happiness that must have made her want to shake me. I was in love, and my man loved me. It was as primitive and as all-enveloping as that!

She said, "*Yes*, Emma. If I hadn't seen how it was between you and Heywood, I would have thrown Darrell at your head. Either way, it doesn't matter much. We need your money."

Her frankness shocked me, for such a person, of such good taste. But a quick look at her before her face turned away, showed me that she was pressed into saying that, pressed by circumstances, and at her last ebb. She went on, "My son Darrell is in trouble and needs big money to get him out. It's as simple as that. I love my son, weak as he is."

"I know that," I told her softly. "That's why you let him come over to the island, and you don't let Heywood know."

She took it that I disapproved of her loyalty to the one, and her lack of loyalty to the other. "You just wait until you're married and you have sons, Emma, before you judge other mothers; before you can possibly *know* how one's loyalty can be torn this way and that. I used to wait for the day when Colin Ketwill died, wicked as that sounds, and you'll never know how I felt when I heard that he had left everything to you."

I nodded. "I think I do know to a certain extent. I've often watched your face, especially when Darrell's around. As Heywood says, I'm inquisitive. I must be. But it's only because I like people."

She said, pausing before she went to fetch him to strap up my ankle, "Are you sure it's Heywood you want, and not my Darrell?"

"Can't you tell?" I countered. "It's been Heywood from the first night he went over the causeway and brought me back, believing me to be a maid from Chighampton, and scolding me every inch of the way. Oh, yes, it's Heywood," I breathed, and then he came in at the open door and she turned away.

He strapped my ankle for me, and then he stayed with me a little. It was such a new thing for us both, to have time and the opportunity to be together, and to realize how we felt about each other. But it wasn't until the next day that he voiced the thought that was worrying him.

"They'll say I'm a fortune hunter, Emma," he said. "Will you mind?"

"No, because you are," I told him, and laughed into his startled face. "Only joking. You can have all the money. I don't want it. You know that!"

He got up. I was so afraid my teasing had gone too far. "Heywood, don't turn away from me!" I cried.

He came back and he looked dreadfully embarrassed, beaten, too. He sat down shaking his head a little, and looking at his locked hands. "No, you don't understand. Darling Emma, it's all either black or white for you. No shades of grey. Circumstances have turned me into the sort of sponger

I've always said my half brother is, and I don't think I shall get over it. Emma — I have to beg of you — to lend me some money. Enough to settle Aurelia in some nice place where they will take care of her. I can't keep on like this, with her here. The anxiety's killing all of us."

He didn't look at me. He just stared at his hands, and then dropped his head into them and I had the shaken feeling that if I could see his face it would be wet. With grief, for having to do what he was doing, for he had torn down the principles of a lifetime and had had to ask a woman for money. It made no difference that that woman was the one he loved, nor that she had so much she would never miss it. He had interfered with the fabric of his life. His principles were all he had left, and now they were gone and he was no better in his own eyes than his half-brother was.

I lay there thinking. I wanted to lend it to him, freely, willingly. No, I wanted to give it to him. All of it. But of course, he didn't want that. I said, thinking, "Why do you want to send her away now, after having kept her here for so long? Is it because of me? My safety you're afraid of?"

"More than that," he said huskily, through his fingers. "She got into a terrible rage last night, after I found her and brought her back, and she smashed almost everything in the flat. Hilda said she wouldn't stay a minute longer. It is these rages that worry me. They get worse. I'm afraid Aurelia will go further than breaking things, if I don't have her . . . settled somewhere. But not just in any place. It's got to be somewhere very nice, too plushy for my empty pockets. Now do you see?"

"Yes, I see now," I said slowly. "But I think I'm going to say no to you, my darling." And as his head shot up and a look of disbelief filled his face, that I could say no after he had abased himself to ask me, I said hastily, "No, wait, let me explain. I don't think it's the answer. I think there's another way, that will help you as well as Aurelia. I think — oh, Heywood, dearest, I don't know how to say this, but I'm sure it's right, I *feel* it's right — I really think you must try operating on her again, to cure her, not to put her away."

I don't know how I found the courage to say that, even loving him as I did. And it was no use. There was an awful scene. Like me, he had a sharp temper and we both flared at each other. He told me I was as selfish as anyone else, and that when I got used to the money I would be insufferable, and I told him that he had always been insufferable and wouldn't improve as the years went by. Finally, having got the last word, I lay back gasping, and because I had uttered the last triumphant word, he looked unforgiving and charged out. I lay crying, smothering my face in the pillow, and went to sleep finally, to dream of his back view going out, towards the cave, to his death.

It was a horrible nightmare. I screamed. I kept on screaming, and then I was awake, and saw who my screaming had brought to the door: Darrell Boyd. "Good grief, little Emma, what a big voice you've got when you like to raise it," he said lazily, taking in the situation at once. "What's the matter, love? Nightmare? Dream the cave fell in on you? That ought to teach you not to go around with those madcap kids."

"It wasn't the children who worried me. It was Aurelia," I said heatedly — very angry that it should be Darrell Boyd of all people who had come to see what was the trouble. "Who let her out? And where is she now?"

He shrugged, and sat on the side of my bed without asking my permission. "Do you really care, love? All you have to do is to write a cheque and she can be whizzed off to some plushy sanatorium where they will see she doesn't do anyone a mischief. Why don't you?"

"That isn't the way," I said again, impatiently this time. "At least someone must try to get her cured. If that fails again, well, then, there will be nothing else, but I think Heywood should try!"

"Good grief! Poor brute, you're going to punish him, aren't you?" Darrell Boyd looked mildly shocked but vastly amused. "You'll be sorry, though, if it comes off."

"*Sorry?*"

"Well, of course. Didn't you know, or are they so keen to get their hands on your money somehow that my dear mother and half-brother haven't told you that he isn't free?"

I lay back feeling the colour ebb from my face. "You mean — you can't mean she's his wife?" I managed at last.

"No, don't be silly — even they wouldn't

go that far. But she's as near it as makes no difference. That was what all the trouble was about, the night she crashed her car and messed herself up and the father of the kids. She and Heywood had been having a frightful row, because she wanted him to marry her and he was resisting as usual. Oh, it's been a thing with Aurelia since she was a tiny tot. Always Heywood — and he didn't even encourage her. He didn't like her even. I suppose that was why she set her heart on getting him." He smiled. "Well, get her cured, and she'll have him to the altar, and there's nothing he'll be able to do about it, because the sympathy of everyone will go against him."

"He won't care — he loves me," I said fiercely.

"Does he? Sure it isn't your money?" Darrell mocked. "I didn't notice much affection for you on Heywood's part before old Ketwill snuffed it and left his fortune to you!"

"You'd better go," I said coldly.

"Sure," he said, easily, and went to the door. Then he came back looking nettled. "Oh, help, she's got out again. Give me an alibi, will you, Emma, when Heywood comes after my blood for not keeping an eye on her? I only sort of half promised to stay with her, but there's a limit to what a chap can be expected to do, in return for a roof and a crust of bread."

So that was why Darrell was being allowed to stay! Because he had said he would watch Aurelia, now Hilda had gone! "I'll give you an alibi if you go after her, and really keep an eye on her," I said angrily. "Don't you see, she might hurt the children?"

"Heywood, much more likely," Darrell said, pulling a face. "Especially if she heard the kids telling him what you found in the cave." He came back. "I say, that reminds me — is it true that you found Roman remains in the cave?"

"I don't know what I found, and I wouldn't tell you before I told Heywood, and anyway, I wouldn't talk to you at this moment — you go and find Aurelia before she does more damage. Don't you understand? Heywood thinks she might be dangerous!"

He laughed. "Heywood probably thinks it would be neater to get her out of the way while he marries you and gets his hands on your money. No, don't throw it, Emma, love — think! She cut up rough when she saw you go swimming with him, I understand, so what do you think she'll do if she catches you two having a cuddle, before or after marriage?"

He offended me so deeply, I almost choked. But he merely laughed and strolled away. I threw back the bed-clothes and swung my legs out of bed. I couldn't stay there a moment longer. I limped to the window and looked out at the grey sea and sky. Gales had brisked up today. The trees on the island were bending their heads before it. Somehow I had to get out there and see what was happening.

Agony as it was to put any weight on the ankle, I had to try. I got dressed somehow and with the aid of someone's ash stick, I limped around. To someone like myself, used to darting about, never still, certainly never slow, I don't know how I got through that awful time, but I couldn't stop what I was doing, for the conviction that something had gone very wrong was gaining ground until it had been in a grip of terror that made me cold all over, and when Mary Abbott came running in, and hardly noticed me limping or that I was out of bed, but was sheet-white in the face, I knew that my fears weren't groundless.

"What is it?" I asked sharply. "Is it Mr Stanton? Something's happened to him, I know it has!"

"Has it?" she gasped. "Well, I don't know about that, miss, but what I came to say was that the waterfall's stopped."

The waterfall's stopped. Three simple little words but when I came to consider them, tried to picture it, that high massive man-made pile of rocks with no water gushing over the top, it made a truly horrific picture.

"But it can't have stopped," I said slowly. "I mean, where is it going if it isn't going over the rocks into the pool?"

"It isn't there, and there's no pool, miss, just a great gaping hole, and if those children get there — where are they, miss?" then she looked at me and said, "Here, should you be on that leg, miss? I thought you were in bed."

"Aurelia's got out," I muttered, hobbling past her. "She was making for the hole in the rocks, at the top of the cave. She was following Mr Stanton."

"*Was* she? Well, that's a funny thing because Mr Stanton's gone to see about the children's boat. My father's just finished it."

Sweat streamed from my forehead with the effort. "Be a dear and go and see if you can find Aurelia — I'll never get far," I gasped.

"Well, if it's all one to you, miss, I'd rather not," Mary Abbott said unashamedly. "I keep my distance from that young lady lately. But I will go and see if I can find Mr Stanton and the others. Funny the house is so quiet."

I got as far as the steps down to the courtyard, and then I had to sit down. My foot was paining me abominably. Now I was really worried. Where were the children? Where was Mrs Boyd and Darrell?

I sat there trying to tamp down my anxiety and the senseless fears that tore through me, but it wasn't any use. And then I heard voices, and footsteps. The children, and Mrs Boyd, who looked sheet-white. She said, "Oh, my dear, what are *you* doing out here? I did think that you, at least, would be safely in bed and out of harm's way."

"Something's happened, hasn't it?" I asked her, and she nodded. The children all clamoured at once to tell me and she couldn't make them stop.

"It's Aurelia. She went to the hole and fell down into the cave and her head — "

"Jenneth!" Mrs Boyd shouted, and the child stopped automatically. "Don't say any more," Mrs Boyd said severely. "Emma's had a nasty shock in that place already." To me, she said, "Aurelia is hurt, but my son is bringing her back. Let me help you into the house."

It was no use. I couldn't put that bad ankle to the ground, and I got the full view of Heywood bringing the crumpled body of Aurelia in. I'll never forget it. I kept saying to myself, you must look! You're going to be a nurse so you've got to get used to it! If the children don't mind, why should you?

But it wasn't the sight of an injured person that made me feel sick to the heart. It was the sight of Heywood's face, and the way he carried her, and the memory of Darrell's warning. It just could be true that Aurelia's claim on Heywood was so deeply entrenched over the years, that he could forget me at a time like this. Forget me? He didn't even see me. He didn't see anyone. He just marched unseeingly ahead, carrying her in as he had carried me not so long ago, only this, I fancied, was a little different. Aurelia had been on his hands for a long time, and the very sight of her perpetually reminded him of that day of disaster when he had last operated. And now this to happen . . .

The helicopter came out, with a stretcher to take her back. I asked the children how it had got sent for so soon, and Sheldon said that Darrell had gone over in the small power boat, to telephone an emergency call.

Heywood went with them. His mother said, "How long will you be gone, dear?" and I could see that she was filled with anxiety at the thought of his going into a hospital again after so long away from it.

His answer surprised me no less than it did her. He said, "Ask Emma — she knows," and then he was gone.

She looked at me, but I could only shake my head, the tears running down my face.

Did it mean he was going to operate? Just because of what I had said to him? I put it to her, and she said, "Oh, my dear, what a risk you took, taunting him about not operating. He will have forgotten so much. What will happen if she . . . " but she remembered in time not to go on. The children were listening.

Jenneth said, "Is Aurelia going to die?" and Timmy said, "She's all right in the roof flat, isn't she? What's she want to die for?"

I put my arm round him. He was such a little shrimp of a boy and so gallant. Jenneth leaned against me on the other side and I put the other arm round her, but I wasn't looking at them; I was looking towards the shore as I said to Mrs Boyd, "It doesn't seem to me to matter very much if Aurelia does die. She won't know a thing about it. But Heywood's life depends on it. I think if he does operate, he'll stay there and go on. It's his life. He is only half a man hidden on this island and writing books about Roman times."

"You do love him, don't you?" she said, as if assuring herself on a point that had bothered her.

"You don't, do you, Emma?" the children took her up indignantly.

"Oh, I fight him, but I think I must love him really," I sighed. "He's a good man," I told the children, "and even if he does tear a strip off you lot occasionally, it really isn't any more than you deserve, you know!" And it was their kind of talk; they understood it, and laughed.

"Want to tell me what happened to Aurelia?" I asked them.

Mrs Boyd looked worried, and Sheldon frowned, but the little ones eagerly told me. "She wanted to see what we'd found when we were down there yesterday. and she thought Mr Stanton had gone down and she said she wanted to throw a rock at him. She's screwy, isn't she?" Jenneth finished.

"No, darling, just a very sick young woman. Perhaps Mr Stanton can make her better." I looked at Mrs Boyd. "I suppose you don't know the extent of the injuries, do you?"

"No, and I wouldn't say, if I did," she said briskly. "Ah, here's my Darrell. Darling, carry Emma upstairs to her bed, will you?" and she insisted, in spite of my protests.

Somehow Darrell had changed since I had seen him last. I couldn't understand it. He seemed to have lost that malicious twinkle, that insulting slow drawl, and I think it was since he had done one or two responsible things to help people today.

He put me down on my bed and looked consideringly at me. "A bit dotty to get up and dress and stagger so far from home, Emma, weren't you?" he commented. "You must be in agony. Have a brandy." I said I didn't want one and that it was too early for him but he wouldn't listen and brought a small one for me and a large one for himself. "Needed that," he said, after he had had his. "I got a full view of the mess Aurelia had made of herself. I was the first to see her, too." He looked at me, eyebrows raised. "He'll operate, you know. You've brainwashed him to, silly girl."

"Why silly?" I demanded.

"Because like I said, she'll get him in the end, and you'll be the loser. Well, I'm a fathead, aren't I, because if he doesn't marry you, then little Darrell can step in. Go on, love, say you'll marry me. I'm not such a bad chap if I'm kept well oiled in the pockets."

I closed my eyes. "No offence, Darrell, but if I can't have Heywood, I don't want anyone else," I said wearily.

"Like that, is it? Poor old you," he said, and drew the eiderdown over me and left me.

It was a horrible day of waiting for news. People came over from the mainland to look at the now dry waterfall and to close in the hollow that had been the pool, and to put safety rails round the top of the cave. Somehow Heywood must have found time to get them started. A group of newspaper men came out and some geologists. Mrs Boyd was plainly puzzled by all this activity until Darrell said that Heywood had asked him to make the telephone calls. It was for our safety. Such a sinister thing as the vanishing of the water might mean anything, and Heywood would have enough on his mind today at the hospital, without worrying about us, and our safety.

Heywood didn't come out of the operating theatre for hours. We didn't know the exact time because the tide was up over the causeway and a very rough sea, too. Gales tore at the island. Mrs Boyd was hard put to it, to put the geologists and other strangers up in the house at short notice. Aurelia's suite was a mess, after her last hysterical outburst. She had broken everything, even the bed, which she had whacked at with ornamental chairs until the beautiful headboards had collapsed. Mrs Boyd told me this with thinly veiled annoyance. Heywood's own money had poured into that suite. I had heard that before.

"Never mind," I said. "Don't worry. What's my money for, for goodness' sake? *You* won't be squeamish about availing yourself of as much of it as you want, will you?"

She looked at me, and took my hand. "Emma, my dear," she began, slowly, shaking her head as if in surprise at herself, "I would have said, a week ago, that I would have taken as much as I could from you, believing it to be technically ours. But I can't say that now. I can't touch your money."

"Heywood can. He asked me for it, for Aurelia," I said firmly. "And I didn't mind a bit, so you can too."

"What my son does, is nothing to do

268

with me, my dear. He loves you and trusts you. If he was hard-pressed enough to ask you, then it only shows how much he cares. But I'm not going to touch a penny of your money so don't try to make me." She smiled. "Colin Ketwill must have taken a strong fancy to you, to leave it all to you, and I think I'm not surprised. You're a dear child, and I'm glad Heywood has someone like you to stand by him."

I couldn't speak, I was too choked.

Heywood didn't come back. Days went by. We got cryptic messages at low tide by telegram, things like 'Things not going badly — dare to hope' and 'If she can hold out, it just might work'. I hadn't expected Heywood to be very forthcoming by telegram nor indeed to be dramatic or triumphant, but when the weather eased out, and my ankle was healed enough for me to get about again, I said firmly that I was going to Chighampton to pick up my car and chauffeur, and to do some much needed shopping, but no one was deceived. They all knew I was going to the hospital. Mrs Boyd looked as if she would like to go, but I think she was afraid of leaving Darrell behind, and anyway, the geologists were still poking around, though the newspaper men had long since left with their story.

Poor old Mr Ketwill's chauffeur was so pleased to see me. We talked about the old man for a while, and I told him about my ankle, and then it was time for me to say what I really wanted — to be driven to St John's.

There it was, but surely it looked a little smaller than when I had last seen it, on the train, when I had met Nolan Pearce? I was amazed. I just couldn't believe it. It had seemed such an enormous building then, and I had seemed so young and untried. I had grown up since then. Was that what loving a man did to one? Or was it the things that had happened to me on Moon Island?

I didn't know. I was shown into Aurelia's private room, but only allowed to stay a few minutes. Her head was heavily bandaged, of course, but her face looked subtly different.

Outside, I said to the ward sister, "Is it possible to know yet if she will be improved?"

"With Mr Stanton's operation?" she said. "Oh, yes, I think we can say yes, but he'll want to tell you himself. What a pity the island isn't connected with the telephone." So she knew that much about us.

She asked if I had recovered from my unpleasant experience in the cave, and she looked curiously at me, remembering no doubt that I had been set to come and be a nurse but had since inherited a fortune. She wasn't going to mention that, so I decided I would.

"Nothing's changed, Sister. I still want to train as a nurse, but Mr Stanton doesn't think it will be possible."

She smiled broadly. "Well, no, I don't suppose it would be worth it, either, for such a short time, my dear," and it was some time afterwards before I realized that the poor woman must have jumped to the conclusion that Heywood and I were going to be married.

I didn't disillusion her. I just wanted to see him. She said, "I'll take you up to Theatre 4 if you like, my dear — he should be out soon."

So we went up in the lift and I looked around me with a sad sense of loss, and what-might-have-been. Colin Ketwill hadn't done me such a good turn, after all, because inheriting all that much money, it just wasn't possible to keep it a secret.

I said I would wait on my own as I had no doubt she was very busy, so she took the hint and left me. Someone else came along, though, and decided, on discovering who I was, to tell me how much they had been indebted to Mr Stanton for helping out, instead of leaving them once his own patient was on the way to recovery. "You knew, of course," he said engagingly, "that Mr Stanton is tipped for a very rosy future. I used to think I'd like to be a brain surgeon myself, but having watched the great man, I think it's a bit of a cheek on my part to aspire higher than a poor old G.P." He was a nice young man, engagingly frank about himself, and with no illusions. I ought to have wanted to talk to him but I didn't. I just wanted to sit there and wait for my first sight of Heywood.

He would come out first, wouldn't he? Leaving the others to finish? Or would he come out last? I didn't know, and it fussed me. If he really was considered a great man, I supposed there would be a bit of protocol about it. In the end he came out walking by the side of the stretcher and we nearly missed each other. Only there was a mirror on the wall, on the angle, to show both ways if someone was coming, like a traffic mirror, and he saw me in it. I saw him at the same time. My heart did a great lift, at the sight of him, still in his theatre cap and gown. He looked so *right*, somehow. And then he had gone on.

Someone else came and more or less forcibly took me into a waiting-room where there were two brand new small armchairs and a new table smelling of new wood, on which were fresh roses in a bowl and a wasp playing about on the tallest one. Brand new magazines lay incongruously by some dog-eared copies of *Punch*, and it all looked pristine neat and tidy. I sat down on one of the chairs and nodded when I was asked if I would like some tea. I didn't know what I was saying. I just kept thinking of that sight of Heywood, and wondering if he would want to go back to Moon Island. It was suddenly all changed. I remembered, looking at a calendar on the wall, that it was almost the end of the school holidays. The children would be gone, too. What would be left? Suddenly I didn't want to go back there either. And then Heywood came in.

He had a dark suit on, and his shirt collar was very, very white against the even tan of his skin. I hadn't noticed that tan on the island.

He stood there for a minute, and I struggled to rise to my feet. Then suddenly he was across the room and had pulled me up the rest of the way and held me fiercely against him.

His face pressed down on the top of my bare head, and he whispered huskily, "Emma, I'm a man again." His voice broke on the last word. "I'm operating, I'm a man again. And you made me." Then he didn't say any more."

But he didn't kiss me, and I did so want him to. He just held me against him, one arm round my waist like a vice, and the other was running up and down the back of my head, and when you do that to shortcut straight hair, it prickles, rather like rubbing a cat's fur the wrong way, and it was all wrong and I was convinced that he was just thanking me for what I'd done before he went back to Aurelia and his life with her.

Of course, I'm hasty. I know it. I was

also near to tears, and not understanding anything. I got away as soon as I could, which wasn't difficult because someone fetched my tea they had promised, and someone else bleeped Heywood and he went, and I didn't get all of what he called over his shoulder.

I went out to the Rolls and had a few words with my chauffeur. He liked to be called John, he said. We discussed what we would do. Things like opening up all the estates and looking them over, and taking on a flat in London, but John wanted first to do a 'nice little world tour' in the Rolls, a thing he had never been able to persuade his late master to do. I said I thought it would be a very good idea, when I could get my hands on the money, and persuade the lawyers to do all the tickets and bookings and things like that. John said he could do things like that. We wrangled pleasantly over it, all the way back to King's Dassett, and he soberly walked me over the again dry causeway, and waited while I made my goodbyes.

At least, that was what I had intended to do, but Mrs Boyd said thoughtfully, "Of course, I've been expecting you suddenly to want to go, Emma, and try out your wings with so much money, but I had rather hoped you would wait till the children went back to school. Then perhaps they won't realize that you're not here. It will be awful for them to have to spend the last few days without you. They'll miss you so," and she looked down at a long letter she had been reading, and slowly packed it up and put it in the envelope.

"The children — oh, I'd forgotten. Of course I can't leave them. But the minute they've gone, I must go," I said.

She agreed with that. "My son has written to tell me about his return to hospital. Did you see him, Emma?"

So I told her what I had seen, but not about my personal meeting with Heywood. She looked at me, and said, "Why don't you have your chauffeur put up in the inn in King's Dassett, and take the children around for the last day or two? You have promised it, and there's no need for secrecy any more, is there?" and she smiled. A doubtful little smile, it was true. I supposed she was feeling rather as if the ground had been cut from under her feet, as I was.

I agreed, and went to tell John, and the children. They were thrilled, of course. "That Macey boy and his beastly father have gone," Sheldon said, with vast satisfaction. "I'm glad they went before we did. It'll be super not having to watch him, because of the dinghy."

"Yes, but it's rotten that so many super places are railed off," Jen said. "Well, I know the people are finding exciting things, but they might let us get a look in. It's our island, isn't it? Well, Mr Stanton's our guardian so that makes his island our home, doesn't it?"

That warmed my heart, except that I kept wondering what it would be like in the future when Heywood married Aurelia, because I didn't know what she would be like, and if she was going to revert to her old wilful self that had caused the death of the children's father, I couldn't see that it would be fine for them.

I made their last few days of the holiday days to remember, and John was taken up as their great friend. He drove us to London and we did the Tower and other well-known landmarks, and Timmy was more thrilled with the Post Office Tower

Restaurant than the Monument. We threw in a few stately homes, the ones that had lions roaming about, although John was rather worried about the Rolls getting scratched. It was I, and not Mrs Boyd, who took them for the odd things to fill up their school lists, and I who replenished their tuck boxes, and then they were gone, and John and I missed them perhaps more than anyone else.

The geologists were waiting for something. It occurred to me, a little too late, that they were waiting for Heywood's return to the island. I should have gone before that happened. Now it was too late. I had left John to get the Rolls serviced, a thing that was an event in his life, so I couldn't do anything about it, and as the geologists were all over the place, there wasn't anywhere private to go and hide, such as the rock-strewn beach I had loved. As a last resort, I went up to Aurelia's flat and hid there.

It was still as she had left it. I wandered about, surveying the damage, and wondering if I should suggest clearing it up before I went. Mary Abbott no doubt had enough to do. I was just at the door, meaning to go down the back way and find her, when Heywood stood there in the opening —

My face reddened and I felt as gauche and awkward as the first day I had come there. He said severely, "Mother tells me you've been agitating to go away, leave the island. Is that true? Did she really have to remind you to wait till the children returned to school?"

I nodded.

"But . . . why?" he asked blankly. "Didn't you want to wait for me to come back? It's your thing, forcing me back into surgery — didn't you want to hear all about it?"

I shook my head. I was biting hard on my lips, and I really didn't know whether I was nodding for yes or shaking for no.

He came slowly over to me and tilted my chin. I pulled my face away. "Don't," I muttered. "or I shall bawl!"

"You usually do when I'm around, darling Emma," he said gently, and took me in his arms and kissed my uncontrollable lips until I had settled quietly. "Now, what's this all about? I've been longing for this moment. Oh, help, the first real kiss, and did it *have* to be here, of all places?

What are you doing up here, anyway? Don't say you want to clean up?"

"I came to avoid you," I snapped.

He put me away from him to look at me. "There must be a good reason for that remark," he said. "It isn't . . . anyone else, is it? That youngster who's going into private practice in Chighampton, the one you met on the train? It isn't him, is it?"

"No." I could just about manage that. "But you're going to marry Aurelia, aren't you? Darrell said so. Everyone said so."

"Did he! Did they indeed!" The old displeasure tightened his face, and then he started to laugh. "You'll never believe this, my dearest, but Aurelia doesn't want me any more.

At that time, I couldn't see Aurelia as anything else but a beautiful form in a private room at St John's with no wishes or desires, not even able to open her eyes. Heywood amplified.

"Come and sit down and let me tell you all about it. She's making slow progress, of course, but we had to move a bone to relieve the pressure," and he paid me the pretty compliment of couching it all in hospital language, technical terms he must have known jolly well were well over my head. But I loved him for it. Somehow I knew dimly that that was as near to nursing as I would get. "And now she's beginning to take notice. She's rather fallen for Sir Jasper — you've heard of him? Ears, nose and throat bigshot? He asked to see the girl wonder after I'd finished with her, and it was the worst mistake the poor chap ever made. She wants him, and she'll get him!" He pulled me into his arms again. "I'll see to that," I thought he said.

Half an hour later, when he pulled me to my feet, all my depression had gone, swept away by an exuberant Heywood. "Mind," he warned me, "I don't promise to be jolly all the time. I'm told I'm rather a taciturn devil. But there aren't many husbands who are perfect. One thing, I haven't got a phobia about all your money — I don't care if people *do* call me a fortune-hunter!" and he kissed me some more. "Besides, I'm likely to be pretty well-off myself. I've kept the best bit for the last, you see. The cave of Black Valerian, my love, thanks to your inquisitiveness, is opening up to be a storehouse of Roman remains. There, how about that?"

And he had to tell me all about it so we sat down again. But at last, hearing our names called from below, for dinner, we got up to go again.

"You said you'd kept the best bit for the last," I reminded him.

"Yes, well, that's it," he said. "Isn't it grand news?"

"Yes, but it's not the best," I said.

"Isn't it? What could be better than that? Oh, I suppose you want to know if I've bought the engagement ring yet? Well, I'm not such a fool, my love. I don't know what you'd like or what your size is. We'll do that together."

I wouldn't move. In the one mirror left unbroken, I could see that my face was swollen and red with crying and my hair an untidy mess as usual, and I was taking a chance, being so uppish about it, but I had to have the thing done properly. After all, this was the big moment in my life. "You haven't asked the question which comes before talk of an engagement ring," I said patiently.

Suddenly he saw what I meant. "Emma, my little love, I never knew you'd stick out for formality," he laughed, kissing me all over again. "Oh, you don't want me to go down on my knees to ask it, do you?"

"No, because I know you wouldn't," I said. "But you could ask me, couldn't you? I would like it, Heywood."

"Well, all right, love — will you? Marry me?"

It wasn't romantic. It was Heywoodish — a bit impatient, brisk, and no doubt his mind was now moving from the happy thoughts of his career in surgery and his Roman remains, towards the pleasant subject of food, but he had asked it, and I was content.

"Oh, yes, darling Heywood," I breathed, "I will!"

BUTTERFLY MONTANE
Dorothy Cork

Parma had come to New Guinea to marry Alec Rivers, but she found him completely disinterested and that overbearing Pierce Adams getting entirely the wrong idea about her.

HONOURABLE FRIENDS
Janet Daley

Priscilla Burford is happily married when she meets Junior Environment Minister Alistair Thurston. Inevitably, sexual obsession and political necessity collide.

WANDERING MINSTRELS
Mary Delorme

Stella Wade's career as a concert pianist might have been ruined by the rudeness of a famous conductor, so it seemed to her agent and benefactor. Even Sir Nicholas fails to see the possibilities when John Tallis falls deeply in love with Stella.

MORNING IS BREAKING
Lesley Denny

The growing frenzy of war catapults Diane Clements into a clandestine marriage and separation with a German refugee.

LAST BUS TO WOODSTOCK
Colin Dexter

A girl's body is discovered huddled in the courtyard of a Woodstock pub, and Detective Chief Inspector Morse and Sergeant Lewis are hunting a rapist and a murderer.

THE STUBBORN TIDE
Anne Durham

Everyone advised Carol not to grieve so excessively over her cousin's death. She might have followed their advice if the man she loved thought that way about her, but another girl came first in his affections.

FATAL RING OF LIGHT
Helen Eastwood

Katy's brother was supposed to have died in 1897 but a scrawled note in his handwriting showed July 1899. What had happened to him in those two years? Katy was determined to help him.

NIGHT ACTION
Alan Evans

Captain David Brent sails at dead of night to the German occupied Normandy town of St. Jean on a mission which will stretch loyalty and ingenuity to its limits, and beyond.

A MURDER TOO MANY
Elizabeth Ferrars

Many, including the murdered man's widow, believed the wrong man had been convicted. The further murder of a key witness in the earlier case convinced Basnett that the seemingly unrelated deaths were linked.

A GREAT DELIVERANCE
Elizabeth George

Into the web of old houses and secrets of Keldale Valley comes Scotland Yard Inspector Thomas Lynley and his assistant to solve a particularly savage murder.

'E' IS FOR EVIDENCE
Sue Grafton

Kinsey Millhone was bogged down on a warehouse fire claim. It came as something of a shock when she was accused of being on the take. She'd been set up. Now she had a new client — herself.

A FAMILY OUTING IN AFRICA
Charles Hampton and Janie Hampton

A tale of a young family's journey through Central Africa by bus, train, river boat, lorry, wooden bicycle and foot.

SEASONS OF MY LIFE
Hannah Hauxwell and Barry Cockcroft

The story of Hannah Hauxwell's struggle to survive on a desolate farm in the Yorkshire Dales with little money, no electricity and no running water.

TAKING OVER
Shirley Lowe and Angela Ince

A witty insight into what happens when women take over in the boardroom and their husbands take over chores, children and chickenpox.

AFTER MIDNIGHT STORIES,
The Fourth Book Of

A collection of sixteen of the best of today's ghost stories, all different in style and approach but all combining to give the reader that special midnight shiver.

DEATH TRAIN
Robert Byrne

The tale of a freight train out of control and leaking a paralytic nerve gas that turns America's West into a scene of chemical catastrophe in which whole towns are rendered helpless.

THE ADVENTURE OF THE CHRISTMAS PUDDING
Agatha Christie

In the introduction to this short story collection the author wrote "This book of Christmas fare may be described as 'The Chef's Selection'. I am the Chef!"

RETURN TO BALANDRA
Grace Driver

Returning to her Caribbean island home, Suzanne looks forward to being with her parents again, but most of all she longs to see Wim van Branden, a coffee planter she has known all her life.

DEAD SPIT
Janet Edmonds

Government vet Linus Rintoul attempts to solve a mystery which plunges him into the esoteric world of pedigree dogs, murder and terrorism, and Crufts Dog Show proves to be far more exciting than he had bargained for . . .

A BARROW IN THE BROADWAY
Pamela Evans

Adopted by the Gordillo family, Rosie Goodson watched their business grow from a street barrow to a chain of supermarkets. But passion, bitterness and her unhappy marriage aliented her from them.

THE GOLD AND THE DROSS
Eleanor Farnes

Lorna found it hard to make ends meet for herself and her mother and then by chance she met two men — one a famous author and one a rich banker. But could she really expect to be happy with either man?

BALLET GENIUS
Gillian Freeman and Edward Thorpe

Presents twenty pen portraits of great dancers of the twentieth century and gives an insight into their daily lives, their professional careers, the ever present risk of injury and the pressure to stay on top.

TO LIVE IN PEACE
Rosemary Friedman

The final part of the author's Anglo-Jewish trilogy, which began with PROOFS OF AFFECTION and ROSE OF JERICHO, telling the story of Kitty Shelton, widowed after a happy marriage, and her three children.

NORA WAS A NURSE
Peggy Gaddis

Nurse Nora Courtney was hopelessly in love with Doctor Owen Baird and when beautiful Lillian Halstead set her cap for him, Nora realised she must make him see her as a desirable woman as well as an efficient nurse.

PREJUDICED WITNESS
Dilys Gater

Fleur Rowley finds when she leaves London for her 'author's retreat' in the wilds of North Wales that she is drawn, in spite of herself, into an old tragedy.

GENTLE TYRANT
Lucy Gillen

Working as Ross McAdam's secretary, Laura couldn't imagine why his bitchy ex-wife should see her as a rival.

DEAR CAPRICE
Juliet Gray

Clifford Fortune married Caprice but his brother, Luke, knew the marriage was a mistake. He could allow himself to love Caprice blindly but that would be betraying his own brother.

IN PALE BATTALIONS
Robert Goddard

Leonora Galloway has waited all her life to learn the truth about her father, slain on the Somme before she was born, the truth about the death of her mother and the mystery of an unsolved wartime murder.

A DREAM FOR TOMORROW
Grace Goodwin

In her new position as resident nurse at Coombe Magna, Karen Stevens has to bear the emnity of the beautiful Lisa, secretary to the doctor-on-call.

AFTER EMMA
Sheila Hocken

Following the author's previous auto-biographies — EMMA & I, and EMMA & Co., she relates more of the hilarious (and sometimes despairing) antics of her guide dogs.

LEAVE IT TO THE HANGMAN
Bill Knox

Dope, dynamite, guns, currency — whatever it was John Kilburn and his son Pat had known how to get it in or out of England, if the price was right. But their luck changed when one of them killed a cop.

A VIOLENT END
Emma Page

To Chief Inspector Kelsey there was no shortage of suspects when Karen Boland was murdered, and that was before he discovered that she stood to inherit substantially at twenty-one.

SILENCE IN HANOVER CLOSE
Anne Perry

In 1884 Robert York is found brutally murdered at his home in Hanover Close. When, three years later, Inspector Pitt is asked to investigate, the murder remains unsolved.

A RARE BENEDICTINE
Ellis Peters

Three vintage tales of medieval intrigue and treachery featuring the author's monastic sleuth Brother Cadfael.

POIROT'S EARLY CASES
Agatha Christie

In this collection of eighteen stories, Hercule Poirot begins his celebrated career in crime.

THE SILVER LINK
– THE SILKEN LIE
Lynn Granger

Elspeth is determined to preserve her Scottish heritage and the Elliot name, but running Everanlea, a large hill farm, presents problems.

THE SONG OF THE PINES
Christina Green

Taken to a Greek island as substitute for David Nicholas's secretary, Annie quickly falls prey to the island's charms and to the charms of both Marcus, the Greek, and David himself.

GOODBYE DOCTOR GARLAND
Marjorie Harte

The story of a woman doctor who gave too much to her profession and almost lost her personal happiness.

DIGBY
Pamela Hill

Welcomed at courts throughout Europe, Kenelm Digby was the particular favourite of the Queen of France, who wanted him to be her lover, but the beautiful Venetia was the mainspring of his life.

SKINWALKERS
Tony Hillerman

The peace of the land between the sacred mountains is shattered by three murders. Is a 'skinwalker', one who has rejected the harmony of the Navajo way, the murderer?

A PARTICULAR PLACE
Mary Hocking

How is Michael Hoath, newly arrived vicar of St. Hilary's, to meet the demands of his flock and his strained marriage? Further complications follow when he falls hopelessly in love with a married parishioner.

A MATTER OF MISCHIEF
Evelyn Hood

A saga of the weaving folk in 18th century Scotland. Physician Gavin Knox was desperately seeking a cure for the pox that ravaged the slums of Glasgow and Paisley, but his adored wife, Margaret, stood in the way.